# The
# Wind Called
# My Name

# The
# Wind Called My Name

## Mary Louise Sanchez

### TU BOOKS

AN IMPRINT OF LEE & LOW BOOKS INC.
NEW YORK

TU BOOKS
an imprint of LEE & LOW BOOKS Inc.
95 Madison Avenue, New York, NY 10016
leeandlow.com

Edited by Cheryl Klein
Book design by Christine Kettner
Typesetting by ElfElm Publishing
Book production by The Kids at Our House
The text is set in Kennerley Roman
with display type in Modern Love and Harman Deco
Manufactured in the United States of America by Worzalla Publishing Company

Tu Books Hardcover ISBN 9781620147801 | 10 9 8 7 6 5 4 3 2 1
FB/NEA Paperback ISBN 9781620149621 | 10 9 8 7 6 5 4 3 2 1
First Edition

FSC
www.fsc.org
MIX
Paper from
responsible sources
FSC® C002589

Library of Congress Cataloging-in-Publication Data
Names: Sanchez, Mary Louise, author. | Sanchez, Mary Louise.
Title: The wind called my name / Mary Louise Sanchez.
Description: First edition. | New York : Tu Books, an imprint of Lee & Low Books Inc., 2018. |
Summary: When ten-year-old Margarita Sandoval's family moves to Wyoming during the Great Depression, she faces racism, homesickness, and the possibility that her grandmother's land in New Mexico may be lost. |
Identifiers: LCCN 2018022777 (print) | LCCN 2018029112 (ebook) | ISBN 9781620147818 (epub) | ISBN 9781620147825 (mobi) | ISBN 9781620147801 (hardback)
Subjects: | CYAC: Family life--Wyoming--Fiction. | Racism--Fiction. |
Hispanic Americans--Fiction. | Depressions--1929--Fiction. | Moving, Household--Fiction. |
Wyoming--History--20th century--Fiction.
Classification: LCC PZ7.1.S2573 (ebook) | LCC PZ7.1.S2573 Win 2018 (print) |
DDC [Fic]--dc23
LC record available at https://lccn.loc.gov/2018022777

*Dedicated to my parents,*
*William Gonzales and*
*Margaret Lucille (Sandoval) Gonzales,*
*for helping us know our deep roots*
*and encouraging us to spread our branches*

# Table of Contents

## A NOTE FOR READERS

*The Wind Called My Name* focuses on a Hispanic
American family in the 1930s, and thus it includes both
words and sayings (dichos) in Spanish and a number of
historical references. If you would like help with or want
to know more about anything you encounter in the text,
please check the list of dichos on page 255 or the glossary
and pronunciation guide beginning on page 257.
Thank you for reading.

## NOTA AL LECTOR

*The Wind Called My Name* se enfoca en una familia
hispanoamericana durante la década de los 1930. Por
lo tanto incluye palabras y dichos en español y varias
referencias históricas. Si necesitas ayuda o quieres saber
más sobre cualquier cosa que encuentres en el texto,
consulta la lista de dichos en la página 255 o el glosario y
la guía de pronunciación que comienzan en la página 257.
Gracias por leer.

## CHAPTER 1

# San Antonio de Padua
## INVOKED FOR LOST ITEMS

**The wooden crosses** at the camposanto were buried in dust as thick as the adobe on our church. I shivered in the cool breeze as the sun came up over the horizon. It was hard to believe we were leaving New Mexico in an hour.

"There he is," my little brother, Ernesto, whispered, pointing to a tall cross.

My older brother, Alberto, took Abuela Rufina's hand and placed it in the crook of his arm as we walked across the road. Mamá and my sister, Felícita, followed behind us. Our family names were carved into many of the wooden crosses in the camposanto. Mamá's Maldonado family was buried close to the road. Papá's Cardenas and Sandoval families were by the far gate. When we got to the grave with a cross for my abuelo, Alberto and Felícita helped Abuela and Mamá kneel. Alberto removed his fedora, like he was in church, and the rest of us bowed our heads.

"Adiós, Andrés, ya me voy a Wyoming," Abuela whispered. "Hasta el cielo, Andrés. Hasta el cielo."

I didn't like thinking of it, but she was right. The next time she'd see our Abuelo Andrés *would* be in heaven. Abuela grasped the cross and kissed it, then blessed the grave like the padre blessed the people at Mass every Sunday.

Alberto helped Abuela to her feet, gathering her and Mamá to his shoulders as they wept. They looked like the winged angels on the tombstones of the new graves. Then we walked over to the plot where our Sandoval and Cardenas family were buried. We bowed our heads before the graves of Abuelo Juan and my great-grandfather José del Carmel Cardenas, who fought in the Civil War. I didn't know when we would see their resting places again.

If I could have collected all our tears as we stood there, the drought that gripped our village would have been over.

I saw Abuelita Cruzita getting out of my uncle's car by the far gate and ran over to her.

"No llores, Margarita," she said, as she put her arm around my shoulder and wiped my tears with her apron. "Tengo un regalo." She handed me a gift wrapped in wax paper from the pocket of her apron. "For my son and you," she said carefully in English.

I smiled through my tears. She was practicing her English. "Please come with us," I said, continuing our conversation in Spanish.

She smoothed my short brown hair around my ears. "You know why I can't. First I must work to pay my taxes for the land."

"Sell the land! Alberto says gringos in Taos want to buy it," I said.

Abuelita pushed her shoulders back. She closed her palm and tapped her chest three times as if she were making a solemn vow. "No. Es mi querencia. The bones of my family are here. I must try to save it. New Mexico is my home—our home. It will always be here for you if you want to return."

I nodded and bit my lip. "How long will it take to save the money?"

"I do not know. The gringos buy my goat cheese and your papá sends money. If I cannot pay, then I will come to Wyoming."

"I'll help you get the money," I said, lifting my chin. "We all will."

Abuelita leaned in and looked me in the eye. "I know you will help. I also honor our name by working. Have pride in our family, Margarita. You promise?"

"I promise, Abuelita."

"You must write and tell us everything." Abuelita's hands were clasped together as if she were praying. "Write in English so we can learn."

My fists tightened. "I will. Write to us too."

She nodded as the rest of the family reached us. We exchanged hugs and kisses. Alberto made room in the back of his car for a box from Abuelita and the basket of food she brought us for the journey. Abuelita gave us her parting gifts: a tin of tobacco for Alberto, rosaries for Felícita and Mamá, a can of marbles for Ernesto, and a jar of capulín jelly for Papá. I opened my present—goat cheese, Papá's and my favorite delicacy. He would be so excited to taste it again.

When it was time to leave, Abuelita Cruzita blessed Mamá, Alberto, Felícita, and Ernesto. She and my abuela Rufina hugged each other and said their goodbyes. One abuela was going and one was staying.

Abuelita made the sign of the cross on my forehead. "Vaya con Dios, Margarita," she said.

"Go with God, Abuelita," I said back to her in English.

Then I slid next to Ernesto and Abuela Rufina in the back seat of Alberto's old 1924 Chrysler, which he had named Claudette after a movie star. We were packed in like snug enchiladas. Alberto turned the key, and Claudette sputtered and wheezed like she was sad to be leaving New Mexico. He pulled a knob, pumped a pedal, and the car started at last.

We were going to Wyoming, where we'd finally be with Papá again after twelve long months. But there was so much we were leaving behind: our land where we herded sheep, our adobe house that we plastered with mud each summer, church fiestas in our village, the smell of piñón wood in the mountains, even my dog, Beto. But most of all, I'd miss our familia, especially Abuelita Cruzita.

I pressed my face to the window and waved until I couldn't see Tío and Abuelita Cruzita anymore.

Claudette kicked up a trail of dust as she moved down the dirt roads. Abuela held her gold-colored statue of Mary, the Queen of Heaven, on her lap, but she should have been holding Nuestra Señora de los Dolores—because it seemed like our hearts too were pierced by swords. No one spoke for miles and miles. Alberto kept clearing his throat, and Mamá had to pass Felícita a handkerchief in the front seat. Tears ran down Ernesto's face, and he wiped his nose on his long-sleeved blue shirt. Abuela patted my little brother's hand. He nodded and smiled.

I rested my head against the car window and studied the colorless New Mexican sky. Maybe the sky would be a beautiful pink or light purple in Wyoming. It might be exciting to see different colored skies on my first trip away from our mountains. Our sky used to be so blue, but in the last few years, it was often as brown as the soil that the wind blew into it. If our land was still good, Papá and Alberto could have grown apples, beans, and potatoes to trade with gente on the other side of the mountain. But we couldn't grow crops with the drought, and last year, Papá finally sold the land to his primo Desiderio from Taos. Papá and Alberto left for Wyoming soon after, and Desiderio let the rest of us stay in the house until we were ready to move. At least now, we were going to be together again, and Papá and Alberto had good jobs on the railroad. We would have money to buy what we needed and to help our familia here.

I had a secret wish for myself in Wyoming too. The mountains made us who we were, but they separated people as well. Everyone in El Carmen, our little village of ten families, was familia by blood or by marriage. My primos had always been my friends, but I thought it was time I had a friend who wasn't my cousin—someone who might find my life interesting, and someone whom I could learn interesting things about.

It was time for me to see what was on the other side of the mountains.

As we turned onto a smoother road, Alberto said, "This is the road I helped build when I worked for Ferra."

I leaned toward the front seat. "Who's she?"

"She? It was a program to help adults get work," Alberto said, drumming on the steering wheel with his fingertips. "F-E-R-A. The Federal Emergency Relief Administration," he said in English.

"Why don't you stay here and work for FERA again?" Felícita said. "Then we wouldn't have to leave."

"They don't have FERA anymore because they ran out of work for us. There's plenty of work on the railroad, thanks be to God."

Mamá spoke up next. "You niños have a chance for a good future in Wyoming. Speak more English. Your papá did this and now he has a good job."

"I don't know English very good," Ernesto said.

"You've all learned more English since Papá and I left last June. Even Abuela," Alberto said.

"Señorita Medina started teaching us English in September," I said. "When she left in January, we got a nun from New York. She made us only speak English. She told us to practice with our families. And we did."

"We all need to practice more and learn," Alberto said. "You don't want to seem foreign in Wyoming."

"Foreign?" Felícita asked. "How could we be foreign? Our ancestors have lived in the United States for over three hundred years."

"If we speak only Spanish, people will think we're foreign. I know," Alberto said.

"What happened, m'ijo?" Mamá said. She touched my brother's hand on the steering wheel.

Alberto grimaced. "When Papá and I first went to Wyoming, we were in the general store talking to each other in Spanish. Two railroaders sitting in the back room called us a bad name. One of them is the bridge tender—Papá and I call him Sueño. Anyway, the word the two men called us reminded me how we have the lowest jobs on the railroad." Alberto took a deep breath. "It will be better for everyone if you speak English and make friends early. Don't make trouble."

Everyone in the car was quiet for a few miles. Then Felícita turned around. "I guess we need to remember one of your favorite dichos, Abuela. 'El que adelante no mira, atrás se queda.'"

I laughed. "Felícita, look at you. You're facing the *back-seat* instead of looking ahead!" Everyone in the car laughed too. Felícita was right. As Abuela's proverb said, we all needed to keep looking ahead and keep learning.

We continued north into Colorado, passing Trinidad, Pueblo, Colorado Springs, and Denver. The towns' names changed from Spanish to English. Sometimes we talked and sometimes we slept or sang. Alberto tried to teach us a song called "I've Been Working on the Railroad," and he sang one called "Beyond the Blue Horizon," which he said he heard on the radio. Alberto, Felícita, and I gave English lessons to Abuela, Mamá, and Ernesto. Claudette guzzled gasoline like our orphaned lambs in New Mexico had guzzled milk. After nine hours, we finally reached the Wyoming border.

The hilly plains in Wyoming stretched to the horizon. There were no tall mountains here, no adobe houses, and the trees were far away in the distance. The grass blew in the wind and we didn't see any people. It made me feel lonely. The sky wasn't pink, purple, or a different color as I'd hoped, but a brilliant blue.

As we traveled through Wyoming, the sun went down, so the sky gradually changed from that robin's egg blue to inky black. Alberto said we wouldn't get to Fort Steele until late at night, so I bunched my sweater into a pillow and drifted off to sleep.

I woke up when I felt hands lifting me out of the car. I was scared for a moment, but then I smelled Mentholatum ointment. Papá!

"Margarita," he said.

I nestled my head against his cheek. It was wet. "Papá."

"You're finally here," he said, kissing my forehead. "I never want to be separated from our family again."

## CHAPTER 2

# La Sagrada Familia
## THE HOLY FAMILY

**The next morning,** a snorting sound startled me out of sleep. Someone or something was breathing hard and shaking the house. I sat up in bed alone. Where was Abuela Rufina? The bed shook and there was a long, loud screeching sound. Was La Llorona trying to take me back to New Mexico? I didn't want to go with the Weeping Woman. "Papá!" I called.

Suddenly, the door opened. Papá ran in, covered my ears with his hands, and hugged me close to him. It was too loud to hear anything, but I could see him mouth the word "train." When he finally lifted his hands from my ears, all I heard was a mournful echo.

"Trains are loud," I said.

Papá nodded. "This house was cheaper than other houses because it's so close to the tracks. After a while, you won't even notice the sounds."

"Is that smell from the train?"

"No. That's the smell of tortillas I'm making." Papá helped me out of bed. "You have *grown*!" he said. "I think you're about as tall as Felícita now."

I stretched to make myself look even taller. "But she's thirteen and I'm only going to be eleven."

He nodded and took my hand, and we followed the smell out of the room and down the hall. "Welcome to your new home, hijita," he said.

I wasn't sure I liked it. Unlike our adobe house in New Mexico, the walls here were wood, with no straw sticking out of them, and there weren't any nichos to hold the statue of Santo Niño de Atocha. The wooden floors seemed bare without rugs.

We walked into a kitchen where Mamá was turning a tortilla on a comal on top of a large black stove. Abuela Rufina, Alberto, and Felícita sat at a long table, while Ernesto stood by the window.

"I'll roll out the rest of the tortillas," Papá said, kissing Mamá on the cheek.

"Buenos días les de Dios, Abuela y Mamá," I greeted them like I did every morning.

"Buenos días te de Dios," they both answered.

Ernesto stretched out his hands as far as he could. "You should have seen it, Margarita! The train was so, so long. It said *U.P.R.R.* on the side." He looked at Alberto. "You always have jobs with letters."

Alberto laughed. "*U.P.R.R.* means Union Pacific Railroad."

I joined Ernesto at the window. I could see the railroad tracks up an embankment past a water pump. "We can wave to you when you're working, Papá," Ernesto said.

"The tracks are long," Papá said. "Alberto and I fix miles and miles of tracks. For now, you can wave to the people on the passenger trains."

Ernesto pouted. "I want to wave to people when I'm eating on the train."

"I hope we all get that wish," Papá said.

When breakfast was ready, Mamá moved newspapers from the table and stacked them on the counter. Felícita and I set the food on the table. We sat down and bowed our heads as Papá said grace. Then he passed around some warm tortillas covered by a flour-sack dish towel.

"This is new," I said. I held my square tortilla up so everyone could see its shape.

Papá smiled. "I made tortillas in the shape of Wyoming to welcome you. And square ones taste better than round ones."

Everyone laughed, and Mamá blinked back what looked like happy tears. Eating breakfast together was like celebrating the end of fasting after Lent. We were a family again.

"Now you can see how busy we've been getting ready for you," Alberto said. "Papá practiced cooking while I was in New Mexico."

Papá dipped his tortilla into the egg yolk. "That's one reason I couldn't go. The garden and the new chickens kept me busy too. Plus, I've been learning all I can to become a section foreman the next time there's an opening. Foremen earn more money. My boss likes my work and I've been here a year, so I could get the job."

"What's a section foreman?" Ernesto asked.

"He's kind of like the mayordomo—the boss," Papá continued in English. "The foreman is the boss of the people who make sure the tracks are in good condition for the trains."

Ernesto nodded. "Ah, the boss of the traqueros."

Papá shook his head and laughed. "You can't keep making a Spanish word out of every English word, but yes, the boss of the tracks." He shook his finger at Ernesto. "Now that we're in Wyoming, I want all of us to try to speak more English. ¿Entiendes?"

I tried to stifle a laugh as I spoke in English. "Then why did you say, 'Do you understand?' in Spanish?"

He laughed as he shrugged. "It sounds better in Spanish!"

"Alberto told us to speak English too," Ernesto said. "He said we won't fit in if we don't. But what if I forget Spanish?"

Alberto put his arm around Ernesto's shoulders. "You won't forget your language. It will always be a part of you. At home we'll keep speaking Spanish most of the time."

After breakfast, Papá poured another cup of coffee for Mamá and Abuela. Felícita and I picked up everyone's dishes and put them in a large basin. "We'll clean those later," Papá said, adding canned milk to his coffee. "Go look around."

We had arrived too late last night to do anything but go to sleep. Now I was ready to see more of our new Wyoming home. Next to the kitchen we found a small bedroom. Mamá's suitcase sat by the door. A mattress with blue-and-white ticking peeked out from the blankets. In New Mexico, Abuela had shared a bed with Felícita, while Papá and Mamá took a mattress out each night for themselves. Now they finally had their own room.

The next room was larger and held the tall bed where Abuela Rufina and I slept last night. Felícita had slept in a small bed against the wall. I stood by my bed and ran my hand along the headboard. The brown spindles were metal, not wood. The dresser wasn't as nice as the ones my tío built and carved, but it was roomy enough for our clothes. Abuela's little gold statue of Mary sat on it, creating an altar. The Virgin wore Abuela's rosary beads draped around her neck.

The third bedroom had two small beds. Alberto's cap hung on one hook on the wall and Ernesto's hat hung on the other. It was like a picture of a dicho I had heard many times: "El hogar es donde cuelgas tu sombrero." In the next room, the parlor looked cold, maybe because it faced an enclosed porch instead of having an adobe fireplace. But once Mamá put our pictures on the wall, it would make the room more welcoming.

I held the screen door open for Felícita and Ernesto. Mamá and Papá followed us. Outside, we saw a big garden with five rows of fuzzy-skinned hava beans about six inches tall. I smiled. We would be eating fresh beans before long and keep dried ones for soup. The ground was covered with the tendrils of pumpkin vines creeping over the garden, each studded with orange blossoms. Mamá lifted some of them, and I saw little nubs on what would soon be tender calabacitas. She rubbed the dirt below some leafy plants. "Beets."

"I know how much you like them roasted." Papá pointed to some delicate ferns. "Carrots are growing there." He bent down and touched some other leaves. "These are turnips."

"This is the biggest garden we've ever had," I said. "We won't be able to eat everything."

"Don't forget we'll can some of the vegetables for winter," he reminded me.

Felícita tore off a few lettuce leaves and popped them in her mouth. "There's enough here to feed all our gente back home. I'm glad these are in the shade so we can grow more all summer long."

We followed the clucking sounds and found chickens and chicks pecking at corn. Ernesto chased the rooster around the yard. Next to a chicken coop, there was a tiny pig in a pen. It was hard to believe we didn't have sheep here. Ernesto might never again be surrounded by a flock, the way so many of our family had been for generations.

Felícita licked her lips. "At least we'll eat good for Christmas this year. Tamales and empanadas will taste better with pork than with some scrawny chicken."

When I turned around, I could see that the brown wooden house had a pitched roof instead of a flat roof like we had on our adobe house. I shaded my eyes to look east. The land was a mixture of rolling hills and plains, dotted with blue-green sagebrush and little else. In the far distance were mountains. There wasn't a church bell tower in sight. For generations, our family had been connected to the church like beads on a rosary. In Wyoming, would we be connected to anyone besides one another?

When we went back inside, we found Mamá standing with her hands on her hips in the parlor, looking at her work. Pictures of our familia now hung on the wall. The sun streamed into the room and made the inlaid straw on the wooden cross look like gold. Our little colorful plaster statue of Santo Niño de Atocha sat on a small blue table covered with a doily that Mamá had crocheted. Pictures of different santos painted on pine board retablos hung on either side of the room.

"It looks really nice," I said. Felícita and Ernesto nodded.

"This looks like a home now," Papá said.

Mamá beamed.

Felícita straightened the frame on the large oval picture of Abuela Rufina and Abuelo Andrés on one wall. Next to it was a smaller picture of our other grandparents. I studied it. "I don't remember having this picture before. It looks like the one in Abuela Cruzita's house."

Mamá folded some newspapers from a big box that sat open on the floor. "It was. But she put it in this box with important papers that she gave us for safekeeping. Felícita, help your papá and Alberto unload the car, por favor, and Margarita, help your abuela to the outhouse after you put this box away. Take it to your room. I think it will fit under the bed for now."

I looked at the room once more. I felt at peace there, just like I did in the church back home.

Abuela waited for me in the bedroom, sitting on a chair. Her rosary beads dangled alongside her long black dress. She smoothed out the creases. Since she was blind, how did Abuela know there were creases in her dress? And how did she keep every hair tucked neatly in her bun?

I couldn't keep my short, straight brown hair from going every which direction, and I could see myself in a mirror. I tucked Abuelita Cruzita's big box under the bed, then helped Abuela Rufina up. She kissed my head.

Outside, Abuela adjusted her shawl around her shoulders before taking my arm again. She took a deep breath of the fresh, cool air. "Ah, qué bueno," she said, patting my hand.

After we left the outhouse, we walked by some big sagebrush. Abuela stopped and took another deep breath. "¿Qué es esto?"

I bent over, broke off a stem off the dry bush, and handed it to her. She sniffed it and held it under my nose. It smelled stronger than the sagebrush at home. "Qué bonito," I said.

"Dime lo que ves," Abuela said.

Ever since she became blind two years ago, she always wanted me to tell her what I saw. "The mountains are far away, but the train tracks are close. The bridge that the train goes over is made of wood and metal. There are no piñón trees, just willows by the river." I sniffled. "There aren't any sheep or churches nearby and it's not home. . . . We lost everything."

She shook her head. "We no lose everything," she said carefully in English. "We are together and this be our new home. Recuerda eso, Margarita. 'No donde naces, sino donde paces.' Ten fe, hijita," she said, as though she could see the future.

Yes, I would keep the faith and believe this move would be good. Our family was together, and I still had hopes of making a new friend.

## CHAPTER 3

## San Pascual
### PATRON OF COOKS AND THE KITCHEN

**We spent the** rest of the day putting our things away and settling in. Soon it started to smell like home, thanks to the aroma of simmering beans in the kitchen.

"I have three eggs here. If you bring me at least three more, we can fix torta de huevos for supper," Mamá said to me. I found a basket hanging on a nail in the porch, and Felícita and I went to gather eggs.

I counted twelve hens scurrying in the yard, and hens sat in two of the seven nests. The hens on the nests cackled. That usually meant they had laid eggs. We walked quietly into the coop and checked the empty nests. Felícita found three eggs. There were no cracks in the eggs and they weren't broken, so she put them in the basket. I wasn't about to risk getting pecked by the hens sitting on the nests, so we left the coop with just the three eggs.

Then I saw a girl walking on the dirt path alongside our house. She seemed to be about ten years old, like me, but she was taller than I was. She wore a floral print dress, a pink sweater, and shoes with a strap on them. She looked as though she had stepped out of the Montgomery Ward catalog. Her hair hung down in ringlets the color of straw, like the inlay on our wooden cross.

I handed the basket to Felícita and ran to meet the girl. When she glanced up, my eyes met her eyes—the color of the sky. Maybe she would be my friend.

"Hello," I said in English. "My name's Margarita."

The girl stopped and spoke slowly. "You from Mex-i-co?"

I shook my head. "No, New Mexico."

"Same thing." She shrugged and pointed to our yard. "Watch out for that hen with the black feathers at the tip of her tail. One day she was outside your chicken coop. When I put her back in, she pecked my hand. Well, I have to go now."

She walked away to wherever she was headed. She looked both directions before she crossed the tracks, but she didn't look back.

*What a strange girl*, I thought. I was trying to be friendly.

Felícita was waiting for me by the chicken coop. "What's her name?"

I shrugged. "She didn't tell me. And she doesn't know geography."

As we washed the eggs in the kitchen, I noticed Mamá had lined up the mason jars of her favorite ingredients in a row on the cupboard shelves. The jars looked like a rainbow, filled with red chile caribe, orange chile pequín, yellow chicos, green dried pumpkins, and blue atole flour.

"Set the table, por favor," Mamá said, speaking in both languages.

Felícita and I set the table with more mason jars for water glasses.

"Felícita, los huevos," Mamá said.

My sister beat the yolks in one bowl, and I beat the whites in another. Mamá folded them together as she melted lard in a skillet. When it was hot enough, she ladled mounds of the puffy egg mixture into the pan. After the eggs browned on the bottom, Mamá gently turned them. They reminded me of how puffed up I was with myself and so sure I'd make a friend quickly.

The kitchen smells made me homesick for our relatives and especially my abuelita Cruzita. But the smells made me feel close to them too. Maybe at that very moment, my tias were making the very same things we were going to eat.

Everyone else was seated when Felícita and I helped Mamá set the food on the table. Then Papá said grace.

"Amén," we all said as we made the sign of the cross.

Ernesto smothered his egg with red chile caribe gravy. "This must be Good Saturday."

Felícita rolled her eyes. "It isn't Lent. You're thinking about Good Friday."

Papá laughed. "No, it isn't Good Friday, but it is a very good Saturday. I could get used to eating like this, but we'll have to watch our supplies of food from New Mexico."

"Abuelita Cruzita gave us some of her food. Will she have enough?" Ernesto asked. "We're not there to help with her land now."

Papá, Mamá, and Alberto exchanged glances. "We still have some family there, and our compadres, the Martínezes, live close by," Papá said. "We'll help her by working and sending money, even if we're here."

We all nodded in agreement.

Alberto cleared his throat. "At least we have it good in Fort Steele. I read in the paper where some mejicanos who live in Worland have to pick sugar beets, if they can get work at all. They're trying to send money home like us. But many of them were sent back to Mexico—even some who were born here in the United States—just because there isn't enough work. The townspeople don't want to help them, especially since Wyoming is hurting from this Depression. They think Mexicans should go back where they came from."

I thought about that girl asking me if I was from Mexico.

Ernesto's eyes welled up. "Will *we* be sent to Mexico? Will Abuelita have to go?"

Alberto patted Ernesto's shoulder. "No. Don't worry. We're not from Mexico, and with Papá and me working, and with everyone's help, we can send money to her and save her land. Who knows? We may want to go back to New Mexico some day."

"And if there's not enough money?" Ernesto asked.

Papá shook his head. "We have to have faith. And maybe I'll get to be the section foreman." Then he changed the direction of the conversation. "Would you niños like to go to the store after supper and buy some kerosene for the lamps?"

"The store's open on a Saturday night?" Felícita asked.

"Mr. and Mrs. Sims are the owners. They reopen the store at sundown after they've had church there during the day."

I sprinkled chopped onions on my beans. "Church on Saturday—in a store? That's different."

"Yes, they're Seventh-day Adventists. Their sabbath is from sundown on Friday to sundown on Saturday. They even bring in a minister from Rawlins. He's kind of like a priest. The owners of the store are doing a big favor for the townspeople by keeping the store open late on Saturday nights. They're closed on Sunday, like most stores," Papá said. He patted his stomach. "Now where is that goat cheese and capulín you brought? I'm ready for dessert."

## CHAPTER 4

# San Miguel Arcángel
## PATRON OF GROCERS

*After supper, Felícita,* Ernesto, and I hurried to wash and dry the dishes, then Papá gave us directions to the store.

"When you cross the tracks, the first thing you'll see is a building that used to be an old army barracks," he said. "A little bit farther, on the other side, you'll see the store." He took some money from his leather coin pouch. "Remember, just get kerosene."

My sister, brother, and I walked along the dirt road where I saw the girl this afternoon. We listened for trains and looked both ways before we crossed over the tracks. We passed the barracks, then saw Sims's General Store. It was bigger than the Ortegas' store in our village in New Mexico. When we opened the screen door, the bells sounded like the little ones we put on the goats' necks at home.

We stepped inside, and I turned around in a circle. This was *nothing* like the Ortegas' store! Tall shelves reached the ceiling behind a counter, but short shelves in the middle separated the long room into what looked like little rooms. A heavy-set man wearing a long white apron stood behind the counter. He had a white beard, which made him look like Abuela Cruzita's billy goat. I noticed his apron was clean. In his store back home, Señor Ortega's apron was usually stained with blood. He became the village butcher after many of the local men left the village to find work and weren't at home to butcher their lambs, goats, or pigs.

This grocer pushed his half glasses up his nose. "Hello. You're new to these parts, aren't you?"

We nodded.

"I'm Mr. Sims. How can I help you?"

"We want to buy kerosene," Felícita said in her best English. Ernesto tugged on Felícita's arm. She bent over to hear him, and he whispered in her ear. Straightening up, she said, "Señor . . . sir, may we look around first?"

"Take your time. I'll be over there." He pointed at the counter. "The missus is in the back too."

We wandered deeper into the store. There were hats with fake fruit on them and skinny books with floppy covers. In one area were some dresses on hangers like someone had just finished sewing them, ready-made for purchase. Mamá had always bought us bolts of gingham at the Ortegas' store to sew us dresses. I saw a pink sweater just like the one the girl wore this afternoon. I looked at the price tag. Two dollars! The girl must be rich.

I caught a glimpse of myself in a long mirror. My dress, which used to be Felícita's, reached just above my knobby knees. My hair looked like Ernesto's, with the same bowl cut. No wonder the girl walked away from me. She probably thought I was a boy.

"Let's see what people in Wyoming eat," I said, pulling Felícita over to some bins.

"I want to see what's making that ticking sound," Ernesto said.

"Go and come right back," Felícita said, like she was Mamá.

We walked over to where canned fruits and vegetables were stacked like short mountains, next to jars of jam and large bags with the words *Arthur's Whole Wheat Flour* stamped on them. Some bins held potatoes, onions, and some wrinkly carrots. It was a good thing Mamá brought some beans and chile from New Mexico, because this store didn't sell them.

Ernesto came back. His eyes were wide. "Come here. See what I found."

We followed him around a shelf into a big open area lined with benches. There was a potbellied stove near a window, some comfortable chairs, and tables covered in coffee cups, ashtrays, and newspapers, like people had left in a hurry. A calendar with a picture of a train hung on the wall, with names written in each day of the week.

On the wall near the side window was a black clock that looked like a cat. The tail was swinging back and forth, and as it swung, the eyes on the cat's head moved back and forth too. I could have told the time with Ernesto's head, the way it moved to the beat of the clock.

I whispered, "This must be someone's parlor, or maybe it's where they have church."

Ernesto frowned. "There's no cross or altar. How could it be a church?"

"No santos either," I said. "Maybe this is what churches are like in Wyoming. Let's look at something else."

We walked back around the shelf. "Look." Ernesto pointed at some marbles, wind-up cars, and dolls. One doll caught my eye. She wore a blue checked dress covered by a thin white pinafore and little white shoes. The doll's auburn ringlets looked like the sheep-gut burrañates Mamá wrapped around her finger before she baked them. The doll cost two dollars. I reached up to touch it.

Felícita pulled my hand back. "No! What if you break it? We need to get the kerosene."

We found a shelf with kerosene, kerosene lanterns, matches, and chicken feed in gunny sacks. I stood on my tiptoes to reach the kerosene. As I brought the can down, I bumped a lantern with my elbow. It tottered on the shelf, and I tried to catch it, but it crashed to the floor and shattered.

I froze. *What have I done?*

A woman rushed over from a room behind the counter. She wore her gray hair pulled into a bun so tight no smile could have escaped.

"You have mon-ey?" she said slowly, raising her eye-brows and voice.

Ernesto's lip trembled and Felícita stared at the wooden floor.

"I'll—I'll clean it up," I stammered in English, as if cleaning up the broken glass might help pay for the lantern.

The woman, who had to be Mrs. Sims, stomped over to the cash register. She jerked a broom and dustpan off a nail on the wall. She shoved the things at me and put her hands on her hips.

After I finished sweeping, she stomped back to the cash register. "Over here," she said. She hit a metal button on the register like it was a whack to my head.

Felícita fumbled in her pocket and handed one quarter to the woman. "Not e-nough. Com-pren-de?" Mrs. Sims leaned across the counter and glared at Felícita, then she opened a black leather book with lines in it. "You need to settle the rest of the bill for the lamp," she said, without breaking the words apart this time. "Who's your papa?" She grabbed a pencil.

Ernesto stood on his tiptoes. "Filadelfio," he said in his biggest seven-year-old voice.

Mrs. Sims put her hands on her hips. "Hmph. Not where are you *from*. What is your father's name?"

"Our papá is Filadelfio Sandoval," I said.

Mrs. Sims sighed and looked up at the ceiling. It was like she was looking to heaven to help her write Papá's name. "P-h-i-l-a-d-e-l-p-h-i-o," she mumbled, writing the letters in the book.

*That's not how Papá spells his name*, I thought, looking at Felícita.

"Spell your last name?" the woman asked.

"S-a-n-d-o-v-a-l," I said.

"That was a nice lamp. You tell your papa the price of that lamp is seven dollars. Now you owe six dollars and seventy-five cents."

Felícita put her hand to her mouth. I gulped. Six seventy-five! Our family didn't have any extra money. What was I going to do?

The bell on the front door jingled, and Mr. Sims came out of the room behind the counter. I turned around. The girl I saw on the road earlier had entered the store. "Hi, Grandma. Hi, Grandpa," she said. She looked at me. "Oh. I saw you this afternoon."

Mrs. Sims stopped writing. "Caroline, this is no time for chitchat. This girl broke a lantern." She pointed to the room behind the counter. "Put an apron on."

The girl named Caroline stood where she was. "I hope you had good luck getting eggs—especially with that mean hen," she said to me.

I nodded and she walked to the other room.

Mr. Sims flipped some pages in the ledger and studied one page. He looked at his wife over his half glasses. "Now, now, Mrs. Sims. Mr. Sandoval will pay us. He's been a good customer."

Mrs. Sims sighed and tucked stray hairs back into her bun. Memories flooded my brain. We weren't always the best customers at the Ortegas' store. The only time Mamá could pay with money was when Papá mailed it to her from Wyoming. Señor Ortega always added any new purchases to our growing bill, then had to wait to get paid. I think Mamá sent me to the store in her place because she was embarrassed to go without money.

Papá needed a good name here in Wyoming. We all did. I clenched my hands and cleared my throat. "We have some chickens and we're growing a garden. Maybe we could pay with eggs and vegetables."

Mr. Sims stroked his beard. "You know, our customers might like some fresh food. We've been so busy with the church that we didn't plant a garden this year. And the train doesn't stop here every day like it used to. Well, Mrs. Sims?" he said, patting his wife's hand. "Since they have chickens, what would you think about them bringing us fresh eggs until their bill is settled?"

Mrs. Sims slipped her apron over her head. "Eggs for now," she said, looking at her husband, but not at us.

"We'll ask our parents and come back as soon as we can," I said, wiping my palms on my dress. Did the chickens lay enough eggs for us to eat *and* pay for the lantern? Now it would take even longer to pay off Abuelita's taxes.

When we left the store, only the bell tinkled a cheery goodbye. I took Ernesto's hand. It was dark, but we could see a small light in the west that gradually grew bigger. Then we heard a sound like a wail. Ernesto squeezed my hand.

"Is it La Llorona?" he asked.

"No, it's a train. Listen to the chug-chug sound," Felícita said. "You know what? We didn't buy kerosene. Oh well. We started paying for the lantern."

As the engine came closer, the rumbling sounded like Mrs. Sims stomping across the wooden floor. Sparks flew from the wheels. We jumped back. I had never seen anything so big as the engine. I felt even smaller than I felt in the store. The train rolled past us so fast that I couldn't have counted the railcars even if I wanted to. But there had to have been at least thirty.

After the train passed, we hurried down the dirt road toward the light from our kitchen window. Felícita held the screen door open, and we went into the kitchen. I stopped short when I saw Mamá, Papá, and Abuela sitting at the table. Papá was counting money and putting it inside a mason jar—probably for Abuelita.

I burst into tears.

"¿Qué pasó?" Mamá asked, stretching out her arms.

"I'm sorry. I'm sorry," I said between my sobs. I told them how I broke the lantern. "Now we won't have that money for Abuelita."

Mamá stroked my hair. "Don't cry, hijita."

Ernesto piped up. "Margarita asked if we could pay with our eggs, and they said yes."

"How many did you get today?" Mamá asked, lifting my chin.

I wiped my tears with the back of my hand. "We got three this afternoon."

"And I gathered eleven this morning," Papá said. "You can take a few eggs to the store each day, but save some para la familia." He stood up and rubbed his eyebrows with his fingers. It was like he was trying to erase from his mind what I had done.

When I went to bed, gentle raindrops pinged on the tin roof. As it got darker, the rhythm of the rain sounded like the crashing glass of the lantern. How was I going to repay the store?

## CHAPTER 5

# Santa Margarita de Antioquía
## PATRONESS OF CHILDBIRTH

**The store was** closed on Sunday, so I couldn't take any eggs and start paying off my debt. Felícita, Ernesto, and I took two paper bags with us as we went for a walk by the river. Alberto had said there was a Catholic church in Rawlins, seventeen miles away, but Claudette needed tires and maybe even a new fuel pump, since the car was leaking gasoline after our long trip. It felt strange not going to Mass, but our family needed to save money, and it would help if we didn't buy gasoline that would just spill on the ground anyway.

Alberto had told us that quelites grew down in the shade of the willow trees. I picked a bunch and took them back to Mamá. After I washed them, she fried some onions, then dumped the quelites in the skillet. The pan spit when the wet greens hit the hot lard. Mamá sprinkled chile pequín seeds over the top like she was baptizing the quelites. We ate them for dinner, and they were delicious.

On Monday morning, before breakfast, I shooed the hens into the yard and fed them. Papá had said not to let the chickens hatch any chicks for a while. If I didn't collect the eggs, the hens might stop laying and start brooding.

I went back inside with the basket. "Mamá, do you want any eggs today?"

"How many did you collect?" she asked, pouring Abuela a cup of coffee.

"The same as we collected Saturday—fourteen."

"Leave me seven and you can take the rest to the store after you eat. Your papá left some money on the table for kerosene."

After a quick breakfast, Ernesto and I left the house. I carried the eggs and the money in the basket in one hand and held his hand with the other.

"Remember, we can't look at anything," I reminded Ernesto. "We're just bringing eggs and buying kerosene."

The bell on the door announced our arrival. I put the basket on the counter.

"Let's see what you got here, little lady," Mr. Sims said. "Why, they're still warm. Better get them in the Frigidaire."

Instead of rubbing each egg with KePeg so they would keep longer, like Señor Ortega used to do, Mr. Sims lifted each egg into an egg carton and put them in the giant icebox. He came back to the counter, took out the black book, flipped to the page that had Papá's name written at the top, and wrote some numbers.

He looked at me over his glasses. "I'm giving you two cents per egg, so that's fourteen cents today. Does that seem fair?"

I nodded.

"Well, it's good doing business with you," he said, shutting the book like it was a signal to end our conversation.

I took the money from my pocket and laid it on the counter. "We need to buy some kerosene."

"I'll get a can for you," Mr. Sims said. He walked over to the aisle where I had broken the lantern yesterday. I focused on holding Ernesto's hand so he didn't wander over to the toys. Mr. Sims came back with a can. "That should do you for a while, little lady. I'll see you tomorrow."

Ernesto and I left the store. I wondered about the Simses' granddaughter, Caroline. We hadn't seen any signs of her today. Was she home? What work did she do in the store? We crossed the tracks and walked into our yard.

"Wait! Wait up," someone shouted just as we were about to open the screen door.

It was Caroline, holding our basket. Her ringlets bounced up and down like bedsprings as she ran toward us.

"You forgot this," she said, extending the basket toward me.

"Gra—thank you. I'm sorry you had to come so far," I said.

"That's okay. It's slow in the store," she said, twirling her dress with her hands. She was wearing a different dress, while I wore the same one she'd seen me in Saturday. "I'm Caroline Sims. I figure you know my grandparents own the store."

"My name is Margarita Sandoval," I said, "and this is my brother Ernesto."

"It's really nice to meet both of you. Grandpa thought you might like me to show you the town."

"I'd like that, but I have to ask first," I said. "Please come in."

She followed us into the parlor and glanced at the pictures on the wall. "Jeepers, you sure have a big family. I've always wanted a big family."

I nodded and fiddled with my dress. "Most are family, but the pictures painted on wood are santos—I mean saints. They're like family too."

"They live there," Ernesto said, pointing toward heaven. "And here," he added as he pointed to his heart.

Caroline scrunched her nose like she didn't under-stand. "What's her name?" She squinted at a retablo my tío painted.

"Saint Barbara," I said. "We ask her to protect our home."

One of Caroline's eyebrows went up. "That's interesting. Don't you ask *God* to bless your home?"

I swallowed. No one had ever asked me that question before. "Yes, but we ask saints to intercede for us too."

She shrugged. "That's really different."

I was glad she didn't say more. "Come and meet our family," I said.

Caroline followed me into the kitchen just as Mamá took a hot, speckled tortilla off the comal. She handed it to Abuela, who set it on a plate and covered it with a flour-sack dish towel. Felícita was peeling potatoes.

"Abuela, Mamá, Felícita, this is Caroline Sims," I said in English. "Her grandparents own the store."

"Welcome," Mamá said in English as well. She wiped her hands on her apron and grasped Caroline's hand.

"Nuestra casa es su casa," Abuela said. She handed Caroline and me hot tortillas.

"Does that mean 'pancake'?" Caroline said, looking at me for the translation.

I smiled. "Abuela, here's your chance to practice English with Caroline."

She cleared her throat. "I say, 'Our house es your house.' I give you tortilla to eat—no pancake," she said proudly.

Caroline smiled and took a bite. "It's good. Thank you, Abuela."

Ernesto snickered. "You just said, 'Thank you, Grandma.'"

She covered her mouth. "I thought that was her name. I already have a grandma."

Everyone laughed, including Caroline. Laughing at one another's jokes and sharing a warm tortilla was exactly how I imagined it could be with a friend.

"Mamá, can we go with Caroline? She wants to show us around," I said.

Mamá nodded and went back to cooking tortillas.

"I don't want to go with two girls," Ernesto said, rolling his eyes.

"You can stay home," I said. "I'm ready."

We left the house. As we walked across the yard, Caroline said, "Your family speaks pretty good English. I thought everyone from Mexico spoke Spanish."

"We're from *New* Mexico," I corrected her. "It's in the United States. We've been learning English for a while, because Mamá and Papá think it's important. We want to try to fit in here. But we still speak Spanish too."

Caroline stopped walking. "Say your name again. I'm not sure I say it right."

"Mar-gar-EET-ah." I said each sound slowly, trilling the r.

Caroline picked up a long stick. "Write it for me."

I formed the letters in the dirt. *M-A-R-G-A-R-I-T-A.*

She studied the letters. "But you said Mar-gar-EET-ah. And your name doesn't have any *e*'s."

"The Spanish alphabet is a little different than the English one."

She scrunched her nose again. "Your name is kind of hard to say. It sounds like Margaret in English. Come to think of it, Grandma has some Marguerite daisies in her flower garden." She pronounced it *Mar-gar-eet*. She started walking and then stopped again. "I have an idea! I could call you Maggie. It's short for Marguerite. Or I could call you Daisy. Either way, you're a flower. Which one do you like?"

"But my name is . . ." I said.

"Which name do you like? Daisy or Maggie?" she asked again, smiling. "Either one will help you have a good, easy-to-pronounce American name."

I scratched the dirt with the tip of my shoe. "Maggie, I guess."

Caroline's face lit up. "Well, Maggie, you'll be blooming this summer, at least in Grandma's garden."

Caroline led me to a camposanto with about fifty graves inside, surrounded by a picket fence. It seemed like weeks since we drove down the dusty road from the camposanto back home. Had it really only been three days? Most of the plots here had wooden crosses with dates engraved on them, but the wood was so weathered, we couldn't read many names. Since there was no church here, there was probably no record of these people. It was almost like their stories were blown away by the wind.

"This is a graveyard for soldiers who fought in the Civil War," Caroline said.

I bent down and touched a cross. "My great-grandfather fought in the Civil War."

"Really?" Caroline said, sounding interested. "This is my uncle's grave. He's a great- or great-great-uncle, I forget exactly what. I don't remember his name either." She laid some dandelions by the marker. "After the Civil War, he came here to protect the men who built the railroad from Ute and Arapaho attacks."

*No wonder the Ute and Arapaho attacked, if the railroad was being built right across their land.* I wondered if any of them remained in the area, like the many different Pueblo peoples who still lived on their ancestral lands in New Mexico. This camposanto was so different from the one at home. We knew everyone who was buried in our family plots.

Caroline and I walked to the newer section of the graveyard. A strong breeze blew through patches of wild grass on the graves and made it seem like the buried bodies were talking to us. She knelt down and pulled some weeds growing by two of the graves. The name engraved on one stone was Mary Alice Sims, who had passed away the year before. I did some quick math. She was only thirty-three when she died. The other, smaller grave had the name Patrick Sims. Caroline stood up and brushed the dirt from her legs.

"Was she your mother?" I asked.

Caroline nodded and pointed to the smaller grave. She closed her eyes for a moment and her chin trembled. "She died after she had my brother. He died a month later."

"My abuelo died last year. He was older than your mother, but it was still hard to lose him," I said.

Caroline smiled, but I noticed her eyes were filled with tears. "Death is always hard. I'm just glad I still have Daddy, Grandpa, and Grandma."

"I know how you feel," I said. And I really did understand how important it was to have family.

"Some days it seems like I know how to get along with Grandpa and Grandma better than with kids my age," Caroline said. "At least you have a sister and brother."

I laughed. "I have an older brother too. He works on the railroad. Sometimes it's easier being with just my abuela."

She picked two dandelions that had gone to seed. "Well, now we have each other. Let's make a wish that we become good friends." She handed me one. "At the count of three, we'll each blow on the dandelion so our wish comes true."

This was exactly what I'd wanted. I closed my eyes as Caroline counted. "One, two, three . . ."

I blew hard and opened my eyes. The wind carried the seeds past the camposanto to grow more dandelions. Maybe our new friendship would bloom just like they would.

As we were leaving, a black-and-white dog appeared on the rise of the hill.

"Here, boy," Caroline called, and the dog wagged its tail.

"Is he yours?" I asked.

"No, but I wish he was. I had a dog named Scooter, but one day he escaped from the yard." She looked down. "Then he got hit by a train crossing the tracks."

My hand instantly covered my mouth. "I'm sorry. Pets are like family."

"Scooter sure was. He kept me company when I didn't have a mother *or* a father."

"Is your father gone?"

"No, but when Mother died, it seemed like he died too, and all I had were Grandpa and Grandma." She sighed and then smiled. "It's better now. Even though he's gone a lot, working for the railroad, when he's home—he's really home. He spends as much time with me as he can." She shook her curls like she wanted to change the subject. "How about you? Do you have any pets?"

"A sheepdog named Beto. I named him after my big brother, Alberto. I wanted to bring him to Wyoming, but we didn't have enough room in the car. Now I'm glad, because he likes to chase things. He would have chased the trains like your dog did. At home he can chase the sheep up and down the mountains all he wants."

As we walked on, Caroline told me about the history of the town. The original fort was named for a Civil War general, Frederick Steele. After the army left, the people in the town, including Caroline's grandfather, bought some of the buildings. We passed the house where my family lived.

"Your house is much newer. It wasn't around when there was a fort here," Caroline said.

I pointed to the three-story house across the road from us with a tall fence around the yard. "Who lives there?"

"The bridge tender. He's supposed to watch to make sure there are no fires in the area, and take care of the bridge so it's safe for trains to cross over. He's always cranky, probably because he doesn't sleep very well."

I remembered that Alberto had mentioned the bridge tender. He called Papá and Alberto a bad name. Just past his house, the land dropped down to where a brick building stood.

"That's the pump house. It's railroad property too. The big pumps in there used to put water in the steam engines. The railroad has other pump houses along the route now, and railroaders take showers here after their shifts."

We ran across the tracks by the bridge. When I looked over, I saw the river. Caroline said it was called the North Platte. Four men dressed in overalls were headed for the store, but I didn't see any women or children outside.

"You see that one man with his railroad cap on crooked? The one who's limping? That's the bridge tender. People call him Sleepy."

"I heard about him."

"I'm sure you did." She rolled her eyes. "When he's not sleeping, he smokes like a train, and I imagine he drinks quite a bit because Grandpa sells him a lot of Schlitz beer."

Every town or village seemed to have one of those men.

Caroline sighed. "To tell you the truth, I feel kind of sorry for him. He used to lay tracks, and Daddy says he was a good foreman. But then he had a car accident last winter and hurt his leg. . . . Well, he couldn't work on the section anymore. Mr. Maroni, the boss, offered him the job of bridge tender, and that's what Sleepy has been doing since February or March." She pointed to the top of his house. "That's the tallest building in town and it has steep stairs. He has to climb up there to see if there are fires on or around the bridge. But I think it must be hard for him with that leg and all."

I nodded. "How many people live in Fort Steele?"

Caroline scrunched her mouth. "I guess about one hundred fifty people—about twenty families."

This was a lot bigger than our little ten-family village.

"That's the old army barracks. Soldiers used to sleep here," Caroline said, pointing to a long, narrow building. "I don't know how they slept so close to the railroad tracks."

"What's in the building now?"

"Mr. Maroni and his family live there, but his wife is in Kansas with their kids now."

We went past her grandfather's store. "This used to be the supply base for the army, so it wasn't too hard to convert it into a store," Caroline said. She raised her hand to block the sun. "See that building west of the store? That used to be the fort hospital. Now it's the schoolhouse. Say, what grade will you be in?"

"Sixth."

"Woody-toot-toot! Ain't that something, Maggie? I'll be in sixth grade too. I know Miss Shugart will let me sit by you, being as I can help you with your English."

I didn't know what *woody-toot-toot* meant, and I didn't want to ask. I may not have had much English in school, but my old teacher, Señorita Medina, always said we shouldn't say *ain't*. She said it wasn't proper English.

"What's the school like?" I asked.

"Well, we have eight grades in one room, and last year we even had two kids in high school. None this year." She scratched her head. "There were twenty-two kids last year.

Our teacher, Miss Shugart, is strict, but she also makes the lessons fun. Another thing—she's really pretty and young."

We came to the river. Caroline pointed upstream. "The Carbon Timber Company plant is over there," she said. "Trees get cut and shaped into ties in the mountains and float down here on the river. Then the company sells the ties to the railroad."

I stood taller. "My papá and brother work on the section. They makes sure the ties are safe for the trains to cross."

"Well, my daddy's an engineer," Caroline said. "He has to work crazy hours any day of the week—whenever the railroad calls him. He drives the train, so that means he has the most important job on the railroad."

I swallowed. How could that be? Papá and Alberto fixed the railroad ties so the trains wouldn't wreck. Their jobs had to be just as important as a train engineer's job.

"Daddy had to work overnight last night, so he's sleeping now. I'm with Grandpa and Grandma today. Guess I should see if they need me at the store," Caroline said. "I'll see you tomorrow when you bring the eggs. Ask if you can stay for a while. Okey-dokey?"

"Okay," I said.

She giggled. "That's not how you say it, Maggie. One more time."

"Okey-dokey," I said, trying not to laugh.

★ ★ ★

That night I wrote to Abuelita Cruzita in English, like we promised.

*June 18, 1934*

*Dear Abuelita,*

*We had a good ride to Wyoming. Wyoming looks like New Mexico, but the mountains seem far away. Alberto says we are on the plains, like the llanos. When you see Enrique, tell him I'm glad we didn't bring Beto because we live next to the railroad tracks and he would chase the trains. We live by a big river called the North Platte. It's bigger than the acequias where I used to play. Alberto said a boy drowned in the river last year.*

*We have a big garden, some chickens, and a pig. Papá and Alberto help us take care of them when they get home from work. Most of the time they work eight hours, but sometimes they work twelve hours, all day long. They also have to work Saturdays and Sundays if there are problems on the tracks.*

*Papá enjoyed the goat cheese with the capulín jelly. Maybe someday we'll have a goat like Blanca.*

*I have a friend. Her name is Caroline. I met her at her grandparents' store. She showed me the town. It* is bigger than our village, but it is still a little town. My new friend is interested in many things. I like that.

I pray you are well. We miss you very much. I hope someone helps you read this letter.

Love,

Margarita

## CHAPTER 6

# Santa Teresa de Ávila
## PATRONESS OF FAITH

**In the next** few weeks, Caroline was at her grand-parents' store almost every day when I brought eggs. We liked to explore the town together after she finished her chores. She had to dust the shelves, help customers find things in the store, clean the back room, and sweep the floor. Since the weather was nice and we both wanted to go outside, I often volunteered to sweep.

Mr. Sims served as the postmaster in town. One day, he handed me a letter from Abuelita.

> *July 15, 1934*
> *Dear Margarita,*
>
> *Thanks to God the family is together. I am busy with Blanca. She give me much milk to make cheese. I sell all my cheese to the artists who paint pictures of our mountains.*
>
> *Learn to swim so you be safe. Your primo say hello. He say Beto help him with the sheep. Your primo*

*Enrique help me with this letter. I am learning English.*

*May God bless you on your saint's day.*

 *Love,*

 *Abuelita*

Abuelita was earning money to keep the family's land. Learning to swim was a good idea. I wondered if Caroline knew how to swim. If she did, she could teach me.

Later that day, I swept the aisle where the toys were so I could look at the doll with the auburn ringlets again. It was next to the thin books Ernesto liked. He said they had talking pictures that told a story. I flipped through one called *Famous Funnies*. It had lots more comics than the ones Caroline showed me in the newspapers we picked up in the backroom—in color, too! When I put it back, I noticed there was a sign by it. It said DIME. Maybe it would talk if I spoke to it.

I tiptoed closer and whispered to a book near the sign, "Ernesto says he likes your talking pictures. Please tell me a story."

Just then Caroline came around the corner. "What are you doing?" she asked.

"The sign says *Tell me*, so I'm asking the book to tell me the story."

She shook her head and squinted. "It doesn't say that."

"Yes it does. Your grandpa must have made the sign in Spanish for my brother. He's always saying the store has books that tell him their stories." I pointed to the sign. "D·I·M·E is how you spell *tell me* in Spanish."

She tickled my nose with the feather duster and started laughing. "Why would we put a Spanish sign in the store? That sign spells D·I·M·E, dime—as in ten cents!"

I turned around and folded my arms. She walked around me and picked up my favorite doll, then pretended to talk as the doll in a high-pitched voice. "It's nothing to be mad about, Maggie. It's really quite funny. Tell me you're not mad."

Even though I wanted to be mad, I couldn't help but laugh at how she silly she sounded. I guess it was also funny that I'd think a book could talk to me. "Okay, I'm not mad."

She fluffed the doll's dress and fussed with its ringlets. "She's purty, ain't she? I think Shirley Temple has got to be the purtiest girl in the United States."

"My sister is pretty too," I said.

She shrugged. "I guess so, but I still say Shirley Temple is purtier. Say . . . she's in a new movie. Have you seen any movies?"

I shook my head. "My brother Alberto said he would take us, but he's been busy."

Caroline put the doll back on the shelf. "Daddy isn't working tomorrow, and he wants to go to Rawlins. He'll be busy at the bank and other places, so he said I could see the new Shirley Temple movie if someone goes with me. It's called *Little Miss Marker*. Oh, and Daddy's paying for whoever I take. What do you say?"

*A movie and Caroline wants to take me!* I wanted to hug her. "I say yes, but first I have to ask Mamá."

"Well, if she says okay, meet me here tomorrow after lunch. You can bring the eggs then," Caroline said.

Mamá said I could go. That night I tossed and turned from excitement. My first movie! Movies must be really good if Alberto named his car after a movie star. My brain played my version of a movie in my head. Maybe dreams were what movies were like.

Caroline was standing on a ladder with the feather duster when I came into the store the next morning.

"Good. You're early. Let me put the eggs in the Frigidaire." She backed down the ladder. After she stored the eggs and wrote the number in the ledger, she shouted, "Daddy, we're ready."

"All right, princess," her father said, coming out of the back room. Young Mr. Sims wore a fedora like Alberto's, but I could see his hair was blonde like Caroline's. He was the image of Caroline's grandfather—without the round belly and glasses.

Caroline turned to him. "Daddy, this is my friend, Maggie."

He put out his hand and shook mine. "Nice to meet you. I know your dad and brother. Good people."

"Thank you."

"Guess we better go," he said, turning to Caroline. "Say goodbye to Grandpa and Grandma."

"Hold still," Mrs. Sims said as she retied the bow on Caroline's dress.

Mr. Sims kissed the top of her head. "Have fun, girls."

When we went outside, Caroline's dad bowed and swept his hand toward the backseat of his car. "Your Model A chariot awaits."

*Caroline is the center of everyone's attention*, I thought as we climbed in the car.

Caroline's father drove us the twelve miles to Rawlins. All the way, Caroline talked and I listened.

"I haven't been to the movies for a while. I like the cartoons and Daddy likes the newsreels, but the best part will be the new movie, the main attraction, with Shirley Temple."

We passed a little town and Caroline held her nose as we went through. "That's the refinery," she said, pointing to the tall silver pipes attached to a big building. They spewed smoke and a rotten egg smell.

"This town used to be called Parco," Mr. Sims said.

"After the Sinclair oil company bought the refinery, it's now—Sinclair." He explained that the steam from the refinery caused the bad smells, but the end results were products like gasoline for cars.

About ten miles later we reached Rawlins.

"You're early for the movie," Mr. Sims said. "How about a short tour of our county seat, girls?"

"Let's show Maggie the Ferris Mansion," Caroline said.

Mr. Sims drove through the main street. Cars were parked in front of the big stone buildings. Mr. Sims tipped his fedora at a building. "That's the Hugus-Ferguson Building. Bought my hat there."

He kept driving north until he stopped near a big house made of pink stone. It had three levels of windows that led up to a tower. People were eating under a covered porch.

Caroline clapped her hands. "This is where the rich Ferris family lives. Everyone calls this the Ferris Mansion. How did they earn their money, Daddy?"

"They mined copper."

"Isn't it pretty, Maggie?"

"Yes. I've never seen a house that big or that pink."

"They got those stones near here, right, Daddy?"

"That's right, sweetheart. Sandstone. Well, we better go so you can get your tickets." Mr. Sims drove down the street and turned right. "Now this is what you call a *big* house," he said, nodding to a building nearby. It stretched from one corner of the street almost all the way to the next corner.

"Who lives there?" I asked.

Caroline laughed. "Prisoners. That's the state prison."

"It must hold a lot of people."

"Yep. That's why it's called the big house." Caroline nudged me. Then we all laughed.

*That's what friends should do*, I thought. *They should laugh with you, not at you, when you don't understand something.*

Mr. Sims stopped at a stop sign and pointed to a church as we turned right at the corner. "That's Saint Joseph's Church. It's a Catholic church."

I nodded and crossed myself. Maybe we could attend Mass here when we got some new tires.

"Straight ahead is the old Presbyterian Church. It was built in the late eighteen hundreds. I'll drop you off there. Watch out for cars when you cross the street," Mr. Sims said.

On the other side of the street, I saw a big redbrick building with a painted sign that read STRAND THEATER. Caroline and I got out of the car and waved to her dad.

"I'll see you girls later. Wait for me in the lobby when it's over," Mr. Sims said through the car window.

The movie theater had three large curved windows at the top. We walked to a tall box in front with velvet curtains pulled back on both sides. A girl about as old as Felícita sat inside the box, behind a little cut-out window over a counter.

"Two tickets, please," Caroline said. She put two dimes on the counter.

The girl took the money and handed two tickets to Caroline. I held the theater door open, and we walked inside.

I felt my eyes grow wide. The floor of this lobby had the biggest rug I had ever stepped on. It was bright red and my feet sank into it. I smelled popcorn, and Caroline and I followed the smell over to a popcorn machine. It was a large glass box with a solid metal rack on the bottom. A silver-colored pot hung from wires on the top and popped corn tumbled from the pot out onto the rack. When the corn stopped popping, a boy opened a door at the back of the glass box and scooped popcorn into little bags. Caroline handed him a dime, and he handed her a bag of popcorn.

There were big pictures all over the walls. One of the pictures was of a very handsome man with dark, slicked-back hair and a small mustache. He had big ears, kind of like mine. I got closer so I could read the name on the picture. CLARK GABLE. Another picture showed Shirley

Temple looking at a lady in a pink dress as horses raced in the background. The title on the picture said LITTLE MISS MARKER. That was the movie we were going to see.

"C'mon, Maggie," Caroline called. "We don't want to miss the cartoon."

I followed Caroline through a dark hallway, then stopped. I couldn't see anything even though my eyes were wide open. Was this the way Abuela felt every day? As my eyes adjusted to the darkness, rows and rows of seats appeared in front of me. More people sat in the seats than the pews in the church in our village could have held. There must have been about one hundred people waiting for the movie to start. Caroline pulled my hand until I followed her to a row in the middle and we sat down.

A heavy red velvet curtain parted in front of us, and a cartoon of a dancing mouse came on the giant screen. I laughed at the funny things he did. Then President Roosevelt talked on what was called a newsreel. He didn't sound the way I imagined. I thought he'd have a rough voice because I had seen pictures of him in a newspaper holding a long cigarette, but his voice was clear and higher than I thought it would be.

After the newsreel ended, everything went dark for a few moments. Caroline poked me in the ribs with her elbow. "The movie's starting," she whispered.

Big boxy letters that read FOX FILM CORPORATION

flashed across the screen, followed by loud music. The movie grabbed hold of me right away. Shirley Temple played a little girl called Martha Jane, who was the daughter of a gambler. He left Martha Jane as an IOU on a twenty-dollar bet, which made me frown. An IOU is called a marker, so Martha got a new name—Marky. Her father bet on a horse and the horse lost its race, so the father killed himself and Marky became an orphan. Now I was crying. She looked about three years old because of her short little dress and her baby-looking curls, and I hoped she'd find a new family. But then some gangsters adopted her, and Marky smiled and sang a song about looking at the funny side of life. I laughed when the gangsters bet on how much Marky weighed.

The gangsters made Marky the owner of a race horse, and I sat up on the edge of the seat and cheered for Marky when she rode it. Other kids cheered too, but I must have been extra loud, because Caroline put her finger to her lips.

"Hush, Maggie, you don't want to be like the boys," she said. "People will laugh."

I scooted back onto the soft seat. The last thing I wanted was to have kids laugh at me. To keep from cheering, I put my hand over my mouth, and before I knew it, I was biting my fingernails. When Marky got bucked off the horse, tears ran down my face again. I tapped Caroline's arm.

"Do you have a handkerchief?" I whispered.

"No," she said, still watching the movie.

I wiped my nose with the back of my hand. Marky had to go to the hospital to get blood or else she would die. By the time she got a new family, the bow on my dress was wet and limp.

Then the movie ended, and people in the theater popped up out of their seats. Caroline stretched her arms, then brought her wrist up so she could look at her watch. "According to Mickey Mouse, we've been here two hours. Daddy should be waiting for us."

We stood up, followed people into the aisle, and went outside.

"Well, what did you think, Maggie?" Caroline asked.

"It was better than I even imagined—better than a good dream! Thank you for bringing me."

"Sure. But you really cried a lot. You know the story wasn't real, don't you?"

I nodded, but the story *felt* real to me. In the movie, all the people ended up taking care of Marky and acted like they were a big family. It was like New Mexico. People in my village called one another compadre or primo, even if you weren't really cousins, and we all took care of one another. Caroline probably couldn't understand that feeling, because all she had were her father and grandparents. *No wonder she's a little bossy sometimes*, I thought. *She's never had to get along with anyone else.*

"Now, Shirley Temple—*she's* real," Caroline continued. "Grandpa said new boxes of Bisquick are going to have bowls and small pitchers with Shirley Temple's picture on them." She laughed. "Guess who's going to be eating a lot of pancakes! How about you? Do Mexican people eat pancakes or know what they are?"

"We're not from Old Mexico," I said. "We're *New* Mexican. And yes, we eat pancakes." *Why wouldn't I eat pancakes? I'm not that different.*

"No need to be so huffy. Hey! I think I know a way to keep it straight in my mind. You can't be an old Mexican because of your age, so that means you're a *New* Mexican." She laughed and nudged me in the ribs with her elbow. "Look. There's Daddy." She waved both arms in the air, and he stopped the car by the church for us.

"How was the movie, girls?"

"It was great—wasn't it, Maggie?"

I nodded. The rest of the ride back to Fort Steele, Caroline told her dad the whole story of *Little Miss Marker*. I listened to them, but I was also thinking that I needed to talk to Felícita.

★ ★ ★

"How was the movie?" Felícita asked when I got home.

"It was a really good story. It had horses and

everything. We also saw a cartoon about a duck named Donald. He wanted to play instead of work, until a wise hen taught him that work is important."

"Well, you're back to the henhouse now, and we need to check these wise hens."

We gathered the eggs and made sure all the chickens were inside the fence. Felícita secured the latch on the gate and started walking toward the house.

"Felícita, wait," I said before we went inside.

She turned around.

"I want to ask you something."

"About what?"

"About friends," I said, wringing my hands. "How do you know if someone is your friend? Sometimes I'm not sure Caroline is. She took me to the movie today, but she doesn't seem to care about the things I care about. We always have to do what she wants to do, and sometimes she says things I don't like to hear."

"What did she say?"

"Today she asked if we eat pancakes—as if we're from another planet, like the Mongans in *Flash Gordon*. She acted like I had never heard of pancakes!"

Felícita shook her head. "Tell her I said *she* needs to come down to earth." She motioned for me to sit on the bottom step leading to our porch. Then she sat down next to me.

"What Caroline said was wrong, but put yourself in her shoes. First of all, she's never been around Hispanic people. She probably thinks we're really different from her and doesn't know how we do things. Then she doesn't have brothers or sisters, so she's used to having her way. Plus, she barely knows you—your friendship is really new. You're also the only girl I've seen her with. She might be trying to be your friend the only way she knows how."

"What do you think I should do when I don't like the way she acts?"

Felícita looked me straight in the eye. "I'd give her a chance. She wants to be your friend. That's why she took you to the movies and does other things with you. Remember, friends don't always have to agree with you and be nice all the time. Everyone has a bad day, and sometimes even friends can be cranky. But if she starts to really bother you, stay away for a while. And if she does something that hurts you, you need to tell her what it is so she can try to change." She stood up. "If she doesn't try to change, then she's not a great friend."

I held my head in my hands and sighed.

Felícita extended her hand to me and helped me up. "Keep your chin up. Here's a dicho Abuela used to say when I had problems with my amiga Adelita back home: 'Amigo en la adversidad, amigo de verdad.' You'll know

Caroline is your true friend if she's there for you in good times and bad times. And . . ." My sister smiled and waited for me to finish her sentence.

I smiled back. "I know, I know. If I'm there for her too."

## CHAPTER 7

## San Isidro

## PATRON OF FARMERS AND FARM WORKERS

**The next week** I worked hard to be the kind of friend to Caroline that I wanted to have for myself. Mostly, when she got bossy, I tried to be understanding of what she must feel like every day as an only child with no mother. I couldn't imagine not looking into Mamá's eyes or hearing her voice. Hopefully Caroline would also think about how I felt, living in a town where no one spoke or looked like my family or did things the way we did.

One day, as I was helping Caroline stock Bisquick on the shelves, I studied the ingredients listed in the mix. It had wheat flour, baking soda, salt, shortening, and sugar. Those were the same things Mamá used to make tortillas, except we didn't use sugar, and we used lard instead of shortening. Caroline had shown me the clear blue cup and small creamer with Shirley Temple's picture on them that she got from a Bisquick box. I wanted something with Shirley Temple's picture too. But a box of Bisquick cost twenty cents.

When I got home from the store, I helped Mamá carry the laundry basket outside.

"Mamá, we need Bisquick," I said. I shook out Papá's overalls and handed them to her. "You could make tortillas with it. Bisquick has everything you need to make them—all in one box. It would save time."

"We don't have extra money for things like Bisquick." Mamá clamped clothespins on Papá's overalls.

The wind picked up and an idea breezed into my head. "I think the quelites might be getting taller because of the rain from the other night," I said. "If you don't need me for anything else, I could check on them."

"All right, but don't go too close to the river," Mamá said.

I took the basket in the house, grabbed an empty paper sack, and walked toward the river. The quelites had grown. The stalks were now about nine inches tall with fuzzy, tender leaves smaller than spinach leaves. I stripped the leaves from the stalks. It didn't take long before my paper bag was full. If I could sell them to Mr. Sims, some lucky customer was sure to want the fresh quelites and buy them for supper tonight. With the money, I could buy a box of Bisquick.

Caroline was standing at the cash register when I walked in the store. I placed the paper bag on the counter.

"What's in the sack, Maggie?" Caroline asked. She peeked inside.

"Quelites. They're kind of like wild spinach. I picked them by the river bank. I thought your grandpa could buy them from me and sell them in the store."

Caroline raised her eyebrows and shook her head. "He won't want to buy weeds."

*Weeds?* Quelites weren't weeds. I folded the collar of the bag down, creased it with both hands, and folded it again. "I'll take them home then," I said, and I left.

I thought about what Caroline had said on my way home. Had we always been eating weeds? I didn't think so. This was one of those things Caroline didn't know about me and my family. If she had a chance to taste quelites, she might change her mind.

Mamá opened the sack of quelites when I came home. "We can fix them for supper. Your papá and Alberto will enjoy them."

"They'll both be home?" I asked.

She nodded. "There haven't been any train derailments and the men aren't doing any big projects—just day-to-day repairs near the bridge." She dumped the quelites into an enameled bowl and checked the beans cooking on top of the stove. I took a pitcher outside and pumped water into it. It took me three trips back and forth to the water pump to wash the green leaves clean. I also got some more water for the beans.

The tortilla dough had been resting in a bowl. Mamá was rolling a tortilla out on the table when Papá and Alberto walked in the door with a man.

Papá kissed Mamá on the cheek. "Josefita, I want you to meet our boss. This is Mr. Maroni. As we were coming home from the showers at the pump house, we ran into him by the bridge. He said he hadn't eaten dinner yet, so we invited him for supper."

"Welcome to our home," Mamá said. She flicked dried tortilla dough off her hands before offering one to Mr. Maroni. He took off his railroad cap and shook her hand.

"Thank you for the hospitality. Please call me Leo. My wife has the three kids with her in Kansas, helping her parents, so I'm grateful for the offer to eat something besides sandwiches." He let go of Mamá's hand and looked at everyone in the room.

"Leo, this is my mother," Mamá said as she stood beside Abuela.

Mr. Maroni almost bowed, and in excellent Spanish he said, "Con mucho gusto, Señora."

Abuela nodded and extended her hand. "Nuestra casa es su casa."

Papá nodded in my direction. I spoke up in English. "I'm glad to meet you, Mr. Maroni. My name is Margarita."

Felícita came forward. "I'm Felícita."

Ernesto hung back until Papá gave him a little nudge.

"And who might you be?" Mr. Maroni asked as he squatted down.

"My name's Ernesto."

"I'm happy to make everyone's acquaintance," Mr. Maroni said as he stood up again.

"You can freshen up in the basin by the stove," Alberto said.

"I'll heat some water for you," Felícita said.

"Thank you. It'll feel good to clean off some of this railroad grime."

After he washed, I handed him a face towel. Papá pointed to the parlor, and the men went in to talk before supper.

"Ernesto is going to feed the chickens," Mamá said to me and Felícita. "Help him get them in the coop and then both of you can set the table."

"Do you need anything else, Mamá?" Felícita said.

"Pick some havas and cucumbers too."

The quelites were the last thing Mamá cooked before everyone sat down at the table. Papá said grace and passed the tortillas around the table.

Mr. Maroni helped himself to the hava beans, and the cucumbers and onions in vinegar. "I haven't eaten these beans since my mother was alive. I've always liked fava beans."

Papá put his fork down. "Is that what you call them? We call them havas."

Mr. Maroni cocked his head. "That's interesting. In Italian, we call them favas." He took a bite of the quelites. "My nana used to make a dish like this. Do you have chard in your garden?"

"No, Margarita just picked these today by the river," Mamá said.

"My nana used to put little peperoncino seeds in her dish too," Mr. Maroni said. He took another bite and wiped his mouth with a napkin. "Delicious."

At least *he* appreciated eating weeds.

Mr. Maroni patted his stomach after he finished eating. "Thanks for sharing the great meal. You must have a big garden."

Papá said, "Yes, my wife and our children are good farmers, but I like to brag about my wife's good cooking more."

Mamá blushed.

Alberto cleared his throat. "Abuela, Leo said he used to live in Trinidad, in Colorado." That was where Abuela had lived as a girl.

"It's a nice town," Leo said.

Abuela smiled. "Sí. A very nice town."

"That's where I learned some Spanish."

"What did you do there?" Mamá asked as she got up to ladle more beans in the serving bowl.

"I moved there from Pennsylvania. where I worked in the coal mines, until I decided I liked working aboveground better." We all laughed.

Papá put his fork down. "I like working for the railroad too. Sometimes the hours are long, but at least I can be with the family."

After we finished supper, Felícita and I began washing the dishes. I thought the men would go back to the parlor, but they stayed at the table and continued talking. Mamá poured coffee for herself and the men and sat down to join them.

"I'm really glad you pointed out the dry grass growing alongside the bridge," Mr. Maroni said to Papá. "Like you said, that could cause problems. I don't know why Peter Larsen hasn't said anything or taken care of it."

Papá and Alberto looked as blank as a July blackboard.

"Peter Larsen is the bridge tender," Mr. Maroni said. "Sleepy? Maybe his nickname tells me why the grass isn't cleared. Enough about that. Tell me, Mrs. Sandoval, are you and your family making friends in town?"

She smiled. "Margarita has a good friend—the store-keeper's granddaughter. The rest of us have been busy with the garden and the chickens. Once school starts, our children will make friends, and perhaps I will too."

*Yes*, I thought, thinking about what Caroline said about the quelites. *More friends would be nice.*

On my saint's day, my family sang "Las Mañanitas" to me early in the morning, and later Mamá prepared my favorite dish—chile colorado. Soon it was already August tenth, and Caroline continued to be bossy. I looked for other kids whenever I delivered eggs to the Simses, hoping I might find someone else to be my friend. Usually I'd see boys about Ernesto's age. But there was never a girl my age in the store—except Caroline.

We did have fun together. She taught me how to swim in the river when it ran lower. She came to my house once and ate tortillas, and she liked them so much that she wanted to learn how to cook them herself. I went to her church service a few times, and I was surprised that there was no Communion with the host and wine. We always had it at every Mass. When I asked Caroline about this, she said they only took Communion a few times a year. Caroline also lent me her books. I especially liked reading *Heidi*. Heidi lived in the mountains, like I did in New Mexico. She also played with goats, like Abuelita's goat, Blanca. She seemed like a real person—at least more real than Dick and Jane in the books we used to read in my old school.

"Maggie, do you want to see my new Heidi doll?" Caroline said one day when I met her in the store.

Even though I didn't play with dolls, they were pretty

to look at, so I followed Caroline out of the store and into her grandparents' house. The house was attached to the store, but you had to use a different door to go inside. Caroline had two bedrooms—one at her father's house and this one at her grandparents' house—so she could stay with her grandparents when her father worked overnight.

Caroline took her Heidi doll from the stand it leaned on and handed it to me. Caroline's grandparents had given it to her.

"Her dress is so pretty," I said, as I primped the little lace-edged pinafore the doll wore.

"I'm going to ask for a dress like Heidi's for my birthday," Caroline said. "It's in February. When's your birthday, Maggie?"

"My birthday?" I said.

Caroline tapped her foot. "You know, the day you were born?"

"Oh!" This must be another place Caroline and I used different words for the same thing. "I was born July thirty-first, close to the feast day of Saint Margaret. So, I call the day I was born my saint's day. I'm not used to saying that's my birthday."

She took back her doll. "Well, how *do* you celebrate?"

"On your saint's day, your family sings a song to you in Spanish when you wake up. This year, Alberto even played the song on his guitar."

Caroline placed the doll on the stand. "I never heard 'Happy Birthday' in Spanish. Sing it for me."

"I'll sing the first part." I cleared my throat and sang.

*"Estas son las mañanitas que cantaba el Rey David*
*Hoy por ser día de tu santo, te las cantamos a ti,*
*Despierta, mi bien, despierta. Mira que ya amaneció.*
*Ya los pajaritos cantan, la luna ya se metió."*

When I finished singing, Caroline laughed.

"What's so funny? I don't think I was that bad."

"No, it's just . . . It's not the song we sing. What do the words say?"

"It's about how King David from the Bible sang a morning song, and my family and the birds are singing to me early in the morning because this is my saint's day."

Caroline shook her head. "The kids at school are going to laugh if you sing that song here. You should sing *this* instead." She sang the words "Happy birthday to you" four times, adding my name after the third time. Our song was so much prettier than this one.

"And another thing, don't tell them your birthday is your saint's day. They won't know what you're talking about and they might laugh harder. You need to do what we do here. You're not in Mexico anymore."

"I'm from *New* Mexico, Caroline." *Will you ever learn geography?*

"Whatever. That doesn't matter anyway." She walked away from me and sat on her bed. "What matters is that I'm trying to help you get along in Wyoming. I'm only telling you these things for your own good." Her voice was as soft as the bed she was sitting on. "You believe me, don't you?"

I nodded and swallowed hard. Abuela always said a dicho about the truth being a true friend: "La verdad, aunque severa, es amiga verdadera." Another truth was that our family needed Caroline and her family. If we had friends who said our family worked hard and got along with people in the town, then more people would want to be our friends, and Papá and Alberto had a better chance of keeping their jobs.

Caroline slapped her knees and stood up. "I told Grandpa and Grandma I'd help out in the store, so I better get moving."

I went with her because I actually enjoyed helping out in the store. There were some people waiting at the counter. Caroline helped her grandma by naming the prices of the items, and then her grandma rang up the purchases on the brass cash register faster. I grabbed a broom and swept the floor. When I put the broom away behind the counter, Mr. Sims came over.

"Well, little lady, what do I owe you for your work today?"

I bit down on my lip. "Nothing, Mr. Sims."

"You're always helping out. This time I want to pay you, and I don't want to hear you say no." He opened the cash register and handed me a quarter. *A whole quarter!*

I cleared my throat. "Thank you, Mr. Sims."

"No. Thank *you*. You buy yourself something nice," he said, looking over his half glasses at a display of Big Chief notebooks and pencils. He winked at me. "The pencils only cost a penny."

School would be starting next month. I looked at some of the school supplies, but I really wanted to pay down my debt on the lamp. Once that was paid, I'd put money in the mason jar to help Abuelita Cruzita save our family's land.

Maybe I could earn money another way and keep the quarter for Bisquick. Caroline didn't want the quelites, but I knew she admired our garden. I swallowed. "Mr. Sims, our garden is taking over the back of the house. Would you be interested in buying some vegetables from us? My parents said we have more than enough to can. We also have lots of lettuces."

"Why, that's a wonderful idea. Mrs. Sims is always reminding me how our church wants us to eat healthy, and that includes eating good produce." He winked. "We should sell good produce for others to eat too, before winter comes and there isn't any growing."

"Thank you. I'll bring some vegetables tomorrow when I bring the eggs."

"Well, thank *you* for being a good farmer. They always say, 'The tree is known by its fruits.'"

"But we don't have any fruit trees," I said.

Mr. Sims laughed and patted my shoulder. "It means a man, or in your case a girl, is known by her work." He slapped his hands on the counter. "And speaking of work, I have another little job you might be interested in. People who come to the store read the one newspaper copy I get. By the time everyone's read it, it's old news. I know about ten people who want to buy the newspaper, and the office in Rawlins said they'd send more copies on the train if someone delivered them to the customers."

I nodded. I could do that.

"The paper only comes here twice a week, on Monday and Thursday. Right now the conductor brings it in the depot if anyone gets off the train. Otherwise, he throws it in front of the depot and I pick it up. The delivery person would get the papers and take them to subscribers' homes. Caroline doesn't want the job, and since I know you're a good worker, I thought of you." He picked up some papers and shuffled them around. "They might be able to throw the newspapers on the ground near your house every morning. Three cents a paper, so that's sixty cents a week. What do you think?"

*Sixty cents a week!* "Could I share the job with my sister and brother?" I asked.

"I don't see why not."

I nodded. "When would I start?"

"In about a week. But ask your folks what they think."

"Mamá, Mamá!" I called as I ran in the house. I plunked my quarter on the kitchen table. "Mr. Sims wants to buy our vegetables! And we can deliver newspapers for him too."

She pointed to the chair next to my abuela. "Más despacio, Margarita."

I slowed down and sat in the chair to catch my breath. "Mr. Sims said he would buy vegetables from us—the ones that we don't eat or can."

Mamá and Abuela nodded.

"Then he said the newspaper people in Rawlins need someone to deliver ten newspapers to houses here. He asked me if I wanted to do it." I told them everything Mr. Sims had told me. "He wants to give me sixty cents a week!"

"Creo que es una oportunidad," Abuela said. "Es un santo."

Mamá covered her mouth and laughed. "I agree with your abuela. I think Mr. Sims is a saint too. It does sound like a good opportunity, but you need to ask your papá first."

# CHAPTER 8

## San Gabriel
### PATRON OF MESSENGERS

**The next day,** Ernesto and I carried two large baskets full of vegetables to the store. Mr. Sims opened the door for us, and we placed the baskets on the front counter. His eyes got as round as Little Orphan Annie's in the newspaper as he lifted out the red leaf lettuce. "You mean to tell me Peter Rabbit didn't make a beeline toward your garden?"

Ernesto beamed. "No rabbits made it in our yard."

Mr. Sims held up a hava bean. "Now this is an interesting green bean. I've never seen one this big." He laughed and dangled a few beans in front of Ernesto. "You must have taken these from Jack."

Ernesto looked at me and I looked at Mr. Sims. "We don't know anyone named Jack," I said.

Mr. Sims put his hands on his waist. "What? You don't know the story of Jack and the Beanstalk?"

We shook our heads.

"You ask Caroline for that story. I'm sure she has it.

Well, anyway, this is a strange-looking bean. What do you call it?"

"These are havas." I picked one up and split it open. "We eat the green bean inside like we eat raw peas. Our mamá dries some of them too, and she makes soup out of them in the winter."

"Well, two uses for these beans. That sounds like a good deal." He popped two beans in his mouth. "Pretty tasty too. Now, let's talk about a fair price for all these vegetables. How about one dollar?" Mr. Sims hit a key that opened the cash register.

"We don't want the cash," I said. "We'd rather finish paying for the lantern first."

"If that's what you want," he said. He closed the cash register, then flipped the ledger pages until he got to Papá's name. He wrote down some numbers in the book.

I squeezed Ernesto's hand. "Thank you," we both said.

"Well, what do you know. One dollar on the account brings you up to five dollars, so it looks like we're almost even-steven on the lantern." He pushed his glasses up on his nose. "Your dad is going to be in the black very soon."

Ernesto looked at Mr. Sims. "He can't get in the black. He isn't a fireman on the train."

Mr. Sims laughed from deep in his belly. "'In the black' means you're making money." He turned the ledger around. "See here where I wrote what you owed for the lantern? That's called a debit, and it's what we call being 'in the red.' Now I can add what I pay you in the credit line, where I've been adding your eggs all this time. Once your credits are more than your debits, you're in the black." He reached over and shook my hand and Ernesto's. "Nice doing business with you. By the way, what did your folks say about delivering the newspaper?"

"They said yes," Ernesto said.

"Good. I'll let the newspaper office know they can start sending ten papers next week and your family will be delivering them. And I have a letter here for you too."

"Thank you," I said.

Ernesto and I sat outside on the steps and I read Abuelita's letter out loud.

*August 5, 1934*

*Dear Margarita,*

*We light many candles for you at church close to your saint day. You ask how I learn English. Enrique help me. I learn too from artists who buy my goat cheese. They paint our beautiful mountains. One lady painted my flowers. Her name is Georgia. I do not understand her paintings of my flowers but her heart is good. She helped me with this letter.*

*Love,*

*Abuelita*

Ernesto shrugged. "A flower is a flower, isn't it?"

I folded the letter. "I don't know, but I hope the artists pay Abuelita good for the cheese."

★ ★ ★

The following Monday, early in the morning, I waited on our side of the track as the train passed us, bound for Laramie and Cheyenne. It was funny, but I almost didn't hear the train. I guess I was getting used to the sound. A man threw a gunny sack off the train, and it thumped down next to the tracks. I ran over and untied the sack. Ten newspapers were inside.

Mr. Sims had given me a list of ten houses that wanted the paper, including our own. Papá wanted it to learn more about what was happening in Wyoming, especially about railroad safety laws. After I picked up the papers, I walked around the bridge tender's house and down toward the river. Six houses took the paper in town. I crossed over the tracks to leave a paper for Papá's boss at the barracks and left two at the door of the store. The last paper was for us. It took me about thirty minutes to deliver them all. This job was easier than shooing hens away from their nests and searching for eggs. The next time the papers came, I'd try a different route.

Once I learned the fastest way to deliver the papers, I

shared the job with Felícita and Ernesto. We each had our own mason jar for the money we earned, and we began filling them with the three cents we received for each paper, plus the tips our customers gave us.

By September, our mason jar banks were getting heavy, while our cellar was full of jars of green beans, beets, spiced apples, and sauerkraut from our garden. We continued to sell the vegetables we didn't can or eat to Mr. Sims for a good price. It gave me a warm feeling knowing I was helping to save our family's land.

# CHAPTER 9

## Santa Úrsula

### PATRONESS OF TEACHERS AND SCHOOLGIRLS

**It was finally** the first day of school. I wore my newest dress, which was still a little short, but it had a pocket for my quarter from Mr. Sims. After school, I was going to buy Bisquick. Mamá had said I could spend that quarter however I wished, and I wanted a sugar bowl or creamer with Shirley Temple's picture on it.

Ernesto, Felícita, and I walked together to school. When we got to the schoolyard, Caroline was playing by herself on a swing, even though there were kids everywhere. I wondered why she wasn't talking to the other kids. Maybe she was bossy with them too.

Just as she spied me, a tall woman came out of the school and rang a bell. That must be the teacher, Miss Shugart. Caroline was high up in the air, and the next thing I knew, she jumped from the swing and flew through the air. When she landed, she ran over to meet me.

"This is where we line up," Caroline said, taking my hand and pulling me toward the school. We joined the line by the side of the door with Felícita and Ernesto.

The teacher welcomed each student at the door. When we got to the front of the line, Caroline said, "Miss Shugart, this is my friend, Maggie. Her dad and brother have been working here for a while, and the rest of the family moved here this summer."

"It's nice to meet you," Miss Shugart said. She looked like some of the women in the movie with Shirley Temple, about as old as Alberto, with light brown wavy hair and thin, thin eyebrows. Her lips were as red as the beets that stained my hands when I peeled them. She smiled at me, and then at Felícita and Ernesto. "You must be the rest of the family," she said, shaking Ernesto's hand.

Ernesto stood his ground. "No, I'm Ernesto."

She laughed. "So you are. And who is this pretty girl with you?"

"I'm Felícita."

"What grade are you in?" Miss Shugart asked.

"Eighth grade, Señorita . . . I mean, ma'am."

She smiled again. "Glad to meet you, Fel . . . Well, I'm having a bit of trouble with your name, but I think it translates to Phyllis, so that's what I'd like to call you. And you, young man, can be Ernest."

It was just like Caroline calling me Maggie. Felícita and Ernesto looked at me and I looked at them as if we were strangers meeting for the first time. But Miss Shugart was the teacher, and we needed to fit in here. We nodded and walked into the schoolroom.

It looked a lot like my old school in El Carmen. There were wooden desks in rows on the wooden floor. Pictures of George Washington and Abraham Lincoln in big wooden frames hung next to an American flag. Blackboards wrapped around the west wall of the room, and a potbellied stove sat in the middle.

"Over here, Maggie," Caroline said. She pointed to two desks. They were different than the ones we had in El Carmen. These desks were not attached to one another, and it looked like their tops could open. "Here's the fifth and sixth grade row. So far, it looks like it's just me and you in sixth grade this year." She wiggled into a seat. "Sit here behind me."

I pressed my lips together. I had been hoping there would be some girls my age in town besides Caroline, but it looked like there weren't. I would make the most of it. Ernesto got to sit with the other little kids by the stove where it would be warm in the winter. In fact, he was already talking to his friend, Sam, who he met at the store in front of that crazy cat clock. Felícita sat over by the windows with the older kids.

Miss Shugart came in and stood behind her big wooden desk. When everyone was seated, she picked up some chalk from the tray under the blackboard. In the prettiest penmanship I had ever seen, she wrote her name on the blackboard. "Welcome back, students, and welcome to our new students." She looked at Felícita. "In the eighth grade, please welcome Phyllis." She nodded at Ernesto and then at me. "Ernest is our new second grader, and Maggie is in sixth grade."

The students followed Miss Shugart's lead in clapping for us. That was a nice welcome.

"Let's see who else is here," she said. She read the names of students from first grade to eighth grade from a book. There were five first graders, three second graders, six students in third and fourth grades, two fifth-grade boys, Caroline and me in sixth grade, two seventh graders and three eighth graders. That made twenty-three students in all.

"Please stand for the Pledge," Miss Shugart said. We said the Pledge to the flag and sat down. "Now, this is a poem I'd like us to recite together. I'll try to have one on the board each morning, and soon even the first graders will be able to read it. Then everyone will write the poem in their best handwriting as I start teaching the first and second graders." She took a pointer from the ledge of the blackboard and pointed to the words of the poem as she read it aloud. Then we all read the poem together: "Make new friends but keep the old. One is silver, the other is gold."

*Caroline is my new silver friend*, I thought. Did my cousins count as my gold friends? Were they missing me like I was missing them?

Miss Shugart said, "You'll notice that each section of this large blackboard is dedicated to a certain grade level. I've written the work for each grade level in its own space. You are expected to be good citizens and do your work to the best of your ability. If you finish early, you may always take a book from our classroom library and read that. Older students, I'm hoping you will help the younger students when I need your help." She smiled at us.

"Now I'll work with first graders on writing this poem while the rest of you copy it in your neatest handwriting in your notebooks," Miss Shugart said. "Then continue to do the work for your grade until I meet with you. In the afternoon we'll alternate music and art, and I'll always schedule time to read stories to the entire school."

I looked around the room. The students were all smiling and leaning forward.

The teacher kept talking. "Today I'll start reading *The Adventures of Tom Sawyer* to everyone, and I've got some good reading materials for all the grades. Lunch will be outside, except when it's cold. Are there any questions?" Her eyes moved around the room and no hands went up. "Good. Please start your assignments."

Besides copying the poem, Caroline and I had to copy

about thirty arithmetic problems in our Big Chief notebooks and complete them. There were problems from addition to division. The nuns had taught me well because I even remembered how to divide with two numbers in the divisor.

When it was time for our fifth and sixth grade lesson, Miss Shugart taught us how to write "friendly letters," as she called them. They were really just letters you wrote to people to let them know your news. I guess our family had been writing friendly letters all along and we never knew it. Then she held up a gleaming white tablet of paper, smaller than the Big Chief paper. "Students, the school board somehow found a little extra money for supplies this year. I used some of the money to buy nice stationery paper, because I want you to write a friendly letter to someone and *mail* it."

Caroline turned to me. "We carry that paper in the store. It feels as smooth as linen!"

"Now, you'll want to put that kind of excitement into your friendly letters," Miss Shugart said, smiling. "Write your letter on your notebook paper first, and when I think you're ready, I'll give you a sheet of stationery."

Caroline turned around again and whispered, "I'm writing to Daddy. Who you gonna write to?"

"It's a secret," I said, and licked the lead on my pencil like I'd seen Papá do when he got busy with important papers. I had already written to our familia last week, so I knew exactly who I wanted to write.

In my very best penmanship, I wrote my friendly letter.

*September 4, 1934*

*Dear Shirley Temple,*

*My friend took me to see your movie Little Miss Marker. I really liked it and hope to see more of your movies.*

*My friend's store has Bisquick, and I want to buy some so our family can make tortillas. But the best part of the Bisquick is I can get something with your picture on it.*

*I know you're busy, but I hope you will write back when you can.*

*Your friend,*

*Margarita Sandoval*

I tapped Caroline's back. "Caroline," I whispered. "Will you check my letter and see if it's all right?"

She read the letter quickly. "Underline the name of the movie, and you should sign your name Maggie, not Margarita. And Shirley Temple won't know what this means." She pointed to *tortillas.*

"I'll explain what they are," I said.

"Bring your letter to the store after school. We can fix it there and mail it. I can give you her address and a stamp at the store, and it'll get to Shirley Temple faster." Instead of handing me my letter, she folded it the way Miss Shugart had taught us and put it inside her book.

I really wanted to write Shirley Temple a letter on the pretty stationery, but I didn't want to get in trouble on my first day of school for talking, so I didn't say anything more to Caroline. I did plan to go to the store after school and buy the Bisquick. We could talk then. I tore another sheet of paper from my Big Chief notebook and wrote a letter to Abuelita Cruzita.

*September 4, 1934*

*Dear Abuelita,*

    *We started our new school today. Felícita, Ernesto, and I have new English first names, but I won't let them change our Sandoval name.*

    *See if Señor Ortega sells Bisquick in his store now. Each box has a bowl or creamer with a picture of Shirley Temple. She was in the movie I saw with my friend. You would have liked the movie. It was a good story. I am going to buy Bisquick, and Mamá and I are going to make tortillas with it.*

    *I would like to see the pictures the artists draw of our beautiful mountains. Maybe they will paint your picture.*

    *Love,*

    *Margarita*

Miss Shugart read my letter over my shoulder. She smiled. "Excellent work. Here's your stationery."

I was the first person in the fifth and sixth grades to get a sheet of white stationery, even though Abuelita would get a letter on it instead of Shirley Temple.

## CHAPTER 10

# San Francisco de Sales
## PATRON OF WRITERS AND EDITORS

*After school,* I followed Caroline to the store. "I can fix my letter now," I said.

"I think it's fine," Caroline said. "The train will be coming to pick up the mail soon, so we have to hurry." She got an envelope and stamp from her grandfather. "I've got Shirley's studio address in a movie magazine in my room. While I get it, you should write *Sims General Store* as the return address on the envelope. Grandpa always gets his mail before anyone else in town, and if Shirley writes back, you'll get a letter faster. There's a pencil by the cash register."

Caroline was being bossy, but she was right. I wrote *Sims General Store, Fort Steele, Wyoming* as the return address, but *I* was going to pay for my stamp.

"Okay, I found Shirley's address," Caroline said, coming back from her grandparents' house with the maga- zine. "Go ahead and write it on the envelope so everything is in your handwriting."

I picked up the pencil by the cash register and addressed the envelope. Caroline put my letter inside the envelope, licked the stamp, and slapped it in the corner.

"Now all I have to do is wait," I said. "I hope she'll write back."

"Shirley's very busy, you know. She doesn't write to just anyone."

Caroline wasn't going to spoil my good mood. The mailbox was over by the potbellied stove on the other side of the store. Men sat drinking coffee at the table nearby. They must be railroaders, because they wore the same type of overalls and hat that Papá wore. Maybe they knew him. I dropped the letter in the mailbox, then stopped by the Bisquick display and took a box off the shelf.

"Do you want me to put that on your dad's bill?" Caroline asked as we walked to the counter.

I cringed at the word *bill*, remembering how our bill grew and grew at the Ortegas' store in our village. But Abuela's dicho "Cuando el dinero habla, todos callan" was true for me today. I took the quarter from my pocket and put it on the counter.

Caroline studied it. "Where did you get a whole quarter?"

"I earned it," I said.

"Really," she said, not looking at me. She took a long time to give me change.

"The quarter should pay for the stamp too," I said, picking up the box of Bisquick.

"The letter already has a stamp," she said.

"Keep the change anyway. I've got to go home now."

I walked out the door. It seemed like Caroline didn't believe I could earn a quarter. Did she think I was too poor to have a quarter? Or did she think I *stole* it? At first I felt sad, but then it made me mad that a friend might think this way. If I were like Mamá's pressure cooker, steam would have been coming out my head. I wanted to tell Caroline her own grandfather gave me the quarter, but what would be the use? She wasn't the best listener, and it might make things bad for my family if she didn't believe me. What if Papá and Alberto lost their jobs because Caroline said I was a thief? I had to keep quiet.

The wind picked up, and it reminded me of Abuela's dicho about the wind: "Cuando hace viento, quédate adentro." That was the answer to my problem with Caroline. I should stay close to home and ask Ernesto to take the eggs and root vegetables to the Sims store for a while. Then I would only see Caroline at school.

When I got home, Mamá and Abuela were in the kitchen.

"Mamá, look what I bought!" I grabbed a big bowl from the cupboard and carefully poured the Bisquick into it, looking for my prize. It was like I was sifting dirt to find gold. A little blue bowl tumbled out. I picked it out of the Bisquick and dusted it off carefully.

This was not an ordinary bowl to eat from, but a sugar bowl. It was a clear, deep blue, which Caroline had called cobalt. It also had a picture of Shirley Temple on it.

"Qué bonita," Mamá said as she admired the bowl.

"Can we make Bisquick tortillas for supper?" I said.

"Yes, let's see how they turn out," Mamá said.

"I'll put this away first." I took the bowl to the bedroom Felícita and I shared with Abuela and propped it on a high shelf. Now I could see Shirley Temple's friendly face all the time. *I bet she's nice to everyone no matter who they are*, I thought, *and I bet she'd like to have a Bisquick tortilla*.

Back in the kitchen, Mamá read the ingredients on the box. "This has flour, shortening, salt, baking powder. . . . Yes, it has everything we need to make tortillas. Get a pan and warm some water first."

When the water was warm, she handed the box to me and pointed to the outside of the bowl, a little more than halfway up. "Pour the Bisquick to about here." I did it. "Now add the water," she said. I slowly poured it from the pan. "Now mix it with your hands."

It was a bit dry, so Mamá had me add a little more water. I kneaded the dough for a few moments, then placed a dish towel over the bowl.

"Hace mucho tiempo that I haven't seen your friend," Mamá said as she put the comal on the stove. "I think she would enjoy making tortillas with you, and we know how much she likes them. She should come visit. That way both of you have someone your own age to do things with."

I didn't want to talk about Caroline. "She's been busy with the store." I sprinkled some flour on the big butcher block, then I took the knob of dough from the bowl and rolled it out with the bolillo. Once it was thin and round, I picked up the rolled-out dough and patted it between my palms. The tortilla got even thinner. The final step was to lay it carefully on the hot comal. After a few minutes, I turned the tortilla over to cook the other side.

Before long I had a stack of tortillas about as high as the pancakes pictured on the box. Mamá, Abuela, and I agreed they tasted pretty good.

"We still have half a box left," Mamá said.

"Maybe we could make pancakes sometime," I said.

She smiled and shook her head. "No. It is better for you to teach your friend to make easy tortillas. Ask her to come over tomorrow."

Mamá wanted me to spend time with Caroline. My plan to avoid her was already falling flat—like a tortilla after you roll it out.

★ ★ ★

The next day, Caroline and I walked toward our house after school. "I can't believe the recipe for your tortillas was in the store all along." She giggled. "Come on. I'll race you."

Caroline's cheeks were pink when we got to my house. I hung our coats on the hooks in the porch while she walked right into the kitchen. I heard Mamá and Ernesto greet her warmly, and Abuela was squeezing both of Caroline's hands when I got in the kitchen.

After we washed our hands, we made the dough, then let it rest. When it was ready, Mamá turned to Caroline. "Would you like to try rolling the tortillas out?" she asked.

Caroline nodded. Mamá handed her the bolillo.

"I've helped my grandma make pies, but this rolling pin is so skinny. I've never seen one like this in our store," Caroline said.

"We didn't buy it," I said. "It's made from a broom handle."

Caroline rolled out the lump of dough. She twisted her bottom lip as she concentrated. "Oh, now I see how to do it." When the tortilla was thin enough, she held it up and cocked her head. "This looks like the map of Africa."

"Cook it anyway," Ernesto said.

"Pretty good for your first try," I said.

Caroline made three more tortillas, making them faster and rounder each time. We cooked them on the comal, and she stood taller than usual as she eyed the stack of tortillas we made. "We should taste them now. They say the proof is in the pudding."

"There's no pudding," Ernesto said. "Just tortillas."

She smiled. "That means we just need to see if everything turned out right."

I poked my brother. "You're embarrassing," I said.

Caroline took one tortilla, broke it, and handed everyone a piece, keeping another piece for herself. She looked like a priest at church handing out communion.

"What do you think?" Caroline asked us.

"Very good," Mamá said. Abuela and I echoed her.

Ernesto examined the stack. "They're pretty round too."

"I don't know about that. I'm embarazada," Caroline said.

Abuela and Mamá clapped their hands to their mouths, and Ernesto and I laughed out loud.

"What did I say? Isn't that how you say *embarrassed*? I thought it sounded like Spanish," Caroline said.

I tried hard to stop laughing. "You said 'I'm going to have a baby.'"

Caroline shook her head as she tried not to laugh. She took another bite of her tortilla. "Bisquick tortillas aren't as good as your homemade ones." She looked at Mamá again.

"I told Grandpa how good those are. He said he'd sell your tortillas in the store if you want."

Mamá raised her eyebrows. "It wouldn't be too hard to make some extras."

"We could help, Mamá," said Felícita, "if you want to try."

Mamá nodded, and Caroline rubbed her hands together. "We could give samples away first, and then point people to the stacks of tortillas," she said. "Maybe six tortillas in a stack."

"I could help you with the samples," I said.

"Be sure to tell the people how tortillas are stronger than bread for sandwiches," Felícita said. "And if you roll them up, they take up less room in a lunch bucket."

"And they don't get soggy either," I said.

"All good ideas," Caroline said.

Ernesto tugged at Caroline's dress and smiled. "You can come over and help make them. No one would know which are yours."

Felícita's eyes got big. My hands went to my hips. "You can't expect Caroline to do our work," I scolded Ernesto. "You're learning too much from Tom Sawyer at school." Miss Shugart had just read us a chapter where that naughty boy got all his friends to paint a fence for him.

My brother laughed and pointed to his head. "I like Tom Sawyer."

Caroline laughed too. "I'd be happy to help make tortillas . . . sometimes."

★ ★ ★

Caroline was true to her word, and the next Friday after school, she, Felícita, and I helped Mamá make four dozen tortillas. We wrapped each half dozen in waxed paper. Saturday evening, after the church service, Felícita and I went to the store and saw that Caroline had put a pretty beige tablecloth on a table near the cash register. The tablecloth had a map of Wyoming with colored pictures of things one could find in the state, like Devil's Tower, cows, sheep, bucking broncos, and even Old Faithful.

"I wanted a display here so the customers can taste the tortillas and immediately buy them," Caroline whispered. She arranged the wrapped tortillas around the table and opened one package. She cut each of those tortillas into eighths, like pieces of pie, and piled the pieces on a plate. Next she placed a plate of butter and a knife nearby for the customers. "Since a loaf of sliced bread is a nickel, do you think five cents a dozen is a good price? Three cents for half a dozen? That's what I wrote on the sign."

Felícita and I looked at each other and nodded.

"Here, put these on," Caroline said, handing us each a frilly apron.

Before long, customers started coming in.

"Hello, Mrs. Sanger," Caroline said as she hooked her hand in the lady's arm and led her near the cash register. "We have a new product in the store, and we know how discriminating your tastes are. Won't you have a sample?"

Mrs. Sanger spread some butter on the tortilla and ate it. "That's quite good."

"These are called tortillas. They're the greatest thing since sliced bread," Caroline said.

Mrs. Sanger smiled.

"Your husband might appreciate something new in his lunchbox," I added.

"You could cut Spam strips and roll the tortillas around them," Felícita said. "They would be easier to hold than a sandwich."

"You've convinced me," Mrs. Sanger said, after holding up a package and looking at the price of the tortillas. "I'll take two packages. Put them on the counter. I'll pay when I get the other things I came for."

That evening we sold three and one half dozen tortillas and made eighteen cents.

In the days that followed, the tortillas were so popular that Mr. Sims cleared a shelf in the store for them. Sometimes Caroline even came over and helped us roll them out. The word spread quickly, and soon some of our paper-route customers were asking for them too. I delivered newspapers and tortillas twice a week. My mason jar for Abuelita Cruzita was filling up even faster.

## CHAPTER 11

# San Agustín
## PATRON OF PRINTERS

**The days flew** by like the pages in our new school-books. I liked Miss Shugart, and it turned out we spoke English almost as well as the students who spoke it their whole lives. Maybe it was a good thing our teacher in New Mexico left right after Christmas and we got the new nun from New York. Sister Teresa had made us speak and write in English all day, and Señorita Medina didn't.

In early October we were excited by the letter we received from Abuelita.

*October 6, 1934*

*Dear family,*

*Our Martínez compadres will move to Fort Steele soon. Agustín has a job on the railroad. Esmeralda, Dolores, and Tomás are going too. I will miss their help, but they will be together. Enjoy the foods I send with Agustín.*

*The money I save and the money you send helps*
*me pay my taxes. Do not worry for me. My new friends*
*help me very much.*

*Love,*
*Mamá*

When Ernesto was a baby, Agustín Martínez and his wife, Esmeralda, baptized him. They were his padrino and madrina and compadres to Papá and Mamá. Later that month, they arrived in Fort Steele. They brought their daughter, Dolores, who was Felícita's age, and their little boy, Tomás, who was two years younger than Ernesto. I was the only one who didn't get a special friend from home. They settled in a house across the road from us, close to the bridge tender's house and down by the river.

The Saturday after they arrived, Agustín brought over some food that Abuelita sent from El Carmen—three bushels of fresh green chile, a fifty-pound gunny sack of new pinto beans, and fresh corn on the cob. Mr. Sims didn't sell any of these things at his store, except for corn in a can, and I was excited for all the good food we'd get to eat. But the best things they brought were made by Abuelita Cruzita: another little cheesecloth ball of goat cheese wrapped in wax paper, and a jar of capulín jelly.

"Ay, qué bueno," Papá said as he took the gifts.

Then Agustín opened another small paper bag and

gave Felícita, Ernesto, and me each a pinecone with a few piñón nuts still inside. "Your abuelita just picked these a week ago."

My pinecone was still sticky and it smelled like a pine forest. It made me miss my abuelita and home all the more.

"Hay más piñón," he said, shaking the small bag so we could hear the nuts rattle in it. "But they need to be roasted."

Ernesto looked like a little squirrel shaking his pinecone, especially when he smiled with his new front teeth. "Papá, can we roast the piñón now?"

"We might as well, and then we need to roast this chile before it all turns red. Go gather some twigs while we move some logs."

The men started a fire outside, and I went inside to help Mamá and Esmeralda rinse the chiles. When we were done, Felícita and I carried a large Dutch oven out to the fire. Mamá and Felícita brought the clean chiles, and Ernesto handed the piñón nuts to Papá.

Papá adjusted the grate over the fire and stoked it with a green willow stick. He and Agustín talked about their work on the railroad. "Don't be afraid," Papá told him. "When we see problems, we have to speak up about them, and we need to talk in English. This is for our familia. ¿Entiendes?"

"Yo sé, pero this is Wyoming," Agustín said, pacing in

front of the fire. "Yesterday I was at the store, and I heard railroaders talking about greasers taking all the jobs."

"Greasers?" I said.

"Sí. That's what they call us. We have the lowest jobs on the railroad, just like our gente during the Mexican-American War. *They* greased the wheels on mule carts, while *we* are only allowed to work on the section crews."

Papá's nostrils flared and he shook his head. "It has to change."

Agustín buttoned his jacket and pursed his lips like he was remembering what the railroaders said. "I don't want trouble, but I don't think anything's going to change. You know what the viejitos say: 'Cuando ven un pobre caído todos le dan con el pie.'"

Papá put the large Dutch oven over the fire and shook some of the small brown piñón nuts into the pot. The smell took me back to the mountains, where piñón trees grew near our village. He backed up as some sparks flew. "The viejítos also say, 'Gracia es andar entre las llamas y no quemarse.' That's what we would be doing if I could become a foreman. I'll take us through the flames and we won't get burned." He stirred the nuts like thoughts stirred in my brain.

When the flames went down and the wood was more ashy, Papá threw the ears of corn, which had been soaking in water, on the grate over the fire. He covered them with the large hubcap from Alberto's car. The corn would smoke and dry all day and night.

While Papá was busy, we took the piñón out of the pot and let them cool down. Before we put the smooth piñón nuts in a small brown paper bag, Ernesto and I took a handful of them. After I cracked the shell of each nut, I popped the soft white kernel in my mouth. Ernesto tore off a piece of brown paper sack, and as he cracked each nut, he put the kernels on the paper. Then he ate all the shelled piñón at once.

The rest of the morning, we roasted a bushel of green chile. As the skins blistered, we turned them over to cook on the other side. The smell of roasting chile made Wyoming smell like autumns in New Mexico. I smiled, knowing we were doing the same thing as our family there.

With the other two bushels, Felícita, Esmeralda, Dolores, Mamá, and even Abuela braided the chile together with string to make ristras. I tried too, but the chile kept slipping out of my knots. Mamá pounded some nails outside the house, and we hung the long ristras on them so the sun could turn the chiles bright red. Later, after the chiles dried, Mamá would toast and grind them to make winter meals like red chile with pork or chile colorado—my favorite.

Then we peeled back the husks on the roasted corn to remove the silk, leaving the husks attached so we could make more ristras. I did much better braiding these ristras after my practice on the chiles. We hung the corn ristras in the sun for a couple of days. It was Ernesto's job to check the corn ears to see when they were dry.

One day after school around the end of October, Ernesto ran in the house with two ears. "They're dry. See?" He peeled back the husks and rubbed the cobs together over a dish. The kernels fell right off the cobs.

Felícita nodded. "It's time we get started, then." She took the tub we would use for our upcoming matanza from the porch and brought it in the kitchen. She, Ernesto, and I rubbed all the kernels off the cobs.

"¡Qué bueno. Ahora, una cobija!" Mamá said when we were through. She brought in the woolen Río Grande blanket our abuela Rufina had woven before she became blind. She put the blanket on the table and poured the dried corn kernels carefully in the middle. Felícita and I took two corners of the blanket, and Mamá and Ernesto held the opposite corners. We went outside and gently shook the blanket so that any corn husk mixed in with the kernels could fly away. What was left were chicos, which we would add to the beans.

"Mamá, you promised we could have chicos as soon as they were ready," Ernesto begged.

"It's already four-thirty. The beans will never be ready in time for supper," Mamá said as she gave him a hug.

"We could cook them in the pressure cooker and test that new gasket, Mamá," Felícita said.

Mamá found the gasket and it fit the pressure cooker snugly. We cleaned the new beans and rinsed them and the chicos. In an hour, supper was ready, and we even had time to make fresh tortillas.

"The beans are so pink," Ernesto said, "and the chicos are just right." He took another bite.

"That's because these are new beans," Mamá reminded him.

"I wish we had more goat cheese for dessert," Felícita said as she took her plate to the sink.

"Yum. Goat cheese with capulín. If Abuelita Cruzita comes to visit, she needs to bring Blanca," Ernesto said.

"Why would she bring her goat?" Felícita said.

"So we can have cheese!" Ernesto answered.

"She wouldn't bring Blanca on the train," Felícita said.

Ernesto folded his arms and then unfolded them. "She would . . . if we asked her."

Abuela's hand patted his. "Al que se ayuda, Dios le ayuda."

Ernesto stood up. "That's what I'm going to do. I'm going to ask Abuelita, and I'll bet God will help us find a way."

I pushed my chair back. "I'll help you write a letter to her as soon as we do the dishes."

*October 30, 1934*

*Dear Abuelita,*

   *Thank you for all the food. The goat cheese was so good. If you come, can you bring Blanca? I will ask Papá if she can ride on the train.*

   *Love,*

   *Ernesto*


*October 30, 1934*

*Dear Abuelita,*

   *Thank you for sending us the food. We're glad the money we send is helping you. I especially thank you for the piñón. When I ate the nuts, they reminded me of the places where we used to pick them.*

   *I'm learning about Wyoming in school. The real name of our town is Fort Fred Steele. It was named for a general.*

   *We hope you are well. Tell our tíos, tías, and primos hello for us.*

   *Love,*

   *Margarita*


Ernesto was excited when a letter came about two weeks later.

November 16, 1934

Dear Ernesto and Margarita,

I am glad you enjoy the foods I send. I have many
jars of capulín in the cellar. I sell some to my friends
when they draw pictures of our mountains. My friend
Georgia likes Blanca, but she also like the bones of the
ram's head in my yard. I think she be loca sometimes.

Thank you for working to help me. My jar is heavy
with money. I have hope we will keep our land.

Blanca cost very much to come with me on the
train, and she will have more babies in spring. I pray I
see you in spring or summer.

Love,

Abuelita

## CHAPTER 12

## Santo Tomás

### INVOKED AGAINST BLINDNESS AND DOUBT

**All throughout November,** it felt like we were still in New Mexico. One day it would be cold, and then the next day you almost didn't need a heavy coat. We had a few snow flurries, but we still did not have the kind of snow where our legs sank deep in snow banks. Caroline told me that was coming.

All the vegetables from our garden were canned or sold now, but we continued to make and sell tortillas and to deliver newspapers. I liked helping out, because it kept me from being homesick for our familia back home, but I liked being at school too. I enjoyed listening to Ernesto's lessons about Thanksgiving and learning about the Revolutionary War with Caroline. But I was most interested in the war the seventh and eighth graders were studying.

One day, the week before Thanksgiving vacation, Miss Shugart said to them, "I wonder who had family members who fought in the Civil War, or the War Between the

States, as some people like to call it." She got up from her desk and walked between the rows. "As you know, after the Civil War, some of those soldiers came right here to Fort Steele, to protect the men who built the railroad. Students, raise your hand if someone in your family fought in the Civil War."

I glanced up from my reading to see whose hands went up. Dorothy and Robert in the seventh grade raised their hands. Helen, Joe, Felícita, and Dolores raised their hands for the eighth grade.

"Very briefly, stand up and tell us the name of your relative, the battle he fought at, and where the battle was," Miss Shugart said. "If you don't know all this information, tell us what you do know. We'll start with Joe."

His hands lifted up his suspenders. "Helen's and my great-grandfather fought in Gettysburg, Pennsylvania, at the Battle of Gettysburg. His name was Henry Keiser and he's our mother's grandfather."

"Robert, it's your turn."

"My great-grandfather came from Ohio. He was captured in Georgia and was a prisoner of war. That's all I know."

"Dorothy, tell us what you know."

"William Doolen was my great-great-uncle, I think. He fought the rebels on a ship somewhere in the south. He's buried in Laramie."

"Phyllis, you had your hand raised," Miss Shugart said.

Felícita stood up and said, "Our great-grandfather José del Carmel Cardenas fought for the Union at the Battle of Valverde."

"Where was that, dear?"

"In New Mexico."

Miss Shugart folded her arms. "Are you sure? I never heard of the war coming that far west."

Felícita nodded. "It was the first battle in New Mexico." She started to sit down.

"Were there other battles there?" Miss Shugart said.

Feícita stood tall again. "Yes. Some soldiers from Colorado came down to fight in the Battle of Glorieta Pass. The Union soldiers in New Mexico were able to stop the Confederates there. Otherwise the western states—even California—would have been Confederate."

"Where did you hear this?" Miss Shugart asked.

"Our grandmother Cruzita Cardenas Sandoval told us," Felícita said. "She said our great-grandfather used to tell her stories about the battle."

"Thank you for sharing, Phyllis. Dolores, you had your hand raised."

Dolores stood up. "My great-grandfather fought at Glorieta Pass. His name was—"

"Where was that, dear?"

"New Mexico, like Felícita—I mean Phyllis—said."

Miss Shugart rubbed both her temples with her fingers. "Are you sure?"

Dolores nodded.

The teacher sighed. "Students, put your books aside. It's time for recess."

As we went outside, I overheard Joe laughing. "Do you believe those beaners know anything about the Civil War?" he said to Robert.

Robert shook his head. "*We* know more about the Civil War soldiers. Just look around us. Our relatives came here right after the war."

Caroline was right behind me. "C'mon, Maggie, let's get to the seesaw first," she said. I wondered if she heard Joe. She had to know that "beaner" was a bad name, and my family didn't eat just beans.

I lagged behind Caroline on the way to the playground. We each took a seat on the seesaw. Caroline pushed with her legs and rose into the air.

"If I were in eighth grade, I could have raised my hand when they were talking about the Civil War," she said. "Remember, I showed you where my great-something uncle is buried right here in our cemetery."

"What was his name?"

"I forget. I always have to ask Grandma." She shook her curls back after the wind pushed them in her face. "You know, I don't believe Dolores had someone who fought in the Civil War. She was going to make up a name. How could someone remember the names of people such a long, long time ago?"

"Joe and Dorothy remembered their family," I said, pushing the ground hard with my feet.

"Well, they're smart alecks. What do you expect?"

"What about my sister?"

Caroline shrugged. "Maybe she was trying to act smart too?"

I stopped the seesaw while I was sitting on the ground. Caroline hung high in the air.

"She wasn't trying to act smart," I said. "She was telling the truth. I was there when our grandma told us about her father being in the war."

"You don't have to get so huffy, Maggie. All I know is Miss Shugart is smarter than anyone in the school, and if she never heard of the war being fought where you're from, I believe her."

I stood up and Caroline came down hard. I didn't care. I walked away. She didn't just insult Felícita, she called my sister a liar. She insulted my entire family and our good name.

Miss Shugart rang the bell, and I got in line to go back into the school. I didn't turn around to see if Caroline was behind me. I heard her talking to someone else, so I knew she wasn't hurt.

We went inside and hung our coats on the coat hooks. Caroline came up to me, rubbing her hip. "You should have waited for the bell to ring before you got up from the seesaw. I forgot to tell you, Grandpa's expecting a shipment on the train today. When you bring the eggs tomorrow, ask your mother if you can stay for a while and help unpack it. There might be some fun toys. You could even go to church with me."

I was glad to have a real excuse ready. "I can't this weekend. I need to help out at home. Dolores and Tomás's family and our family are having a matanza."

"A matanza?"

"It's where families get together to kill a sheep or pig. We butcher it and cook some so we all have meat ready for winter."

"We do that in our church when we make jam, but we don't call it a mat-an-za." Caroline struggled to get the word out.

"Well, that's what we call it." I sat down at my desk.

The rest of the afternoon, the fourth, fifth, sixth, seventh, and eighth graders had silent reading in our history books while Miss Shugart gave the first, second, and third graders a spelling test on Thanksgiving words.

"Your first word is *first*," she said. "The English were the *first* people to celebrate Thanksgiving in America."

Felícita was reading her book and twirling one of her

dark curls with her fingers. I waited for her to correct Miss Shugart. *Excuse me, Miss Shugart*, she might say. *The Spanish were the first people from Europe to celebrate an official Thanksgiving.* At our old school we learned the Spanish held a Thanksgiving Mass during their long trip from Mexico to New Mexico in 1598—more than twenty years before the Pilgrims. And of course the Pueblo people gave thanks each day for all living things. But Felícita didn't say anything. Why couldn't *I* say something? I shut my book and sat with my arms folded until Miss Shugart said the words I wanted to hear.

"You're dismissed, sixth grade. Have a nice weekend."

"I'll race you to the swings," Caroline said once we got outside.

"No, I really have to go home. I need to help out with dinner. Oh, and Ernesto will bring the eggs tomorrow morning. I'll be pretty busy." I didn't want to talk to her any more today.

"Okay, guess I'll see you on Sunday?" Caroline said.

"Maybe," I said. I left her behind as I ran to catch up with Felícita and Ernesto. The train's whistle sounded in the distance. When I got my breath back, I asked Felícita, "Why didn't you say something to Miss Shugart during Ernesto's spelling test?"

"About what?" she said.

"About the first Thanksgiving."

"I don't know that much about the Pilgrims," Felícita said.

"I'm not talking about the Pilgrims. I'm talking about what Señorita Medina told us, about Juan de Oñate giving thanks near the Río Grande."

Felícita glared at me. "If Miss Shugart didn't know about New Mexico being a battleground during the Civil War, what makes you think she'd know about Juan de Oñate?"

The wheels of the train clacked toward us on the rails. I shouted over the noise, "You still should have told her."

Felícita shouted back. "You could have told her yourself, and I don't need to prove anything to anyone and get our family in trouble." Sparks flew from her mouth like the sparks from the train.

I closed my eyes and kicked some rocks. She was right. I could have said something, but I didn't. I never spoke up to Caroline either. Life was so much easier in New Mexico. There, people knew their family history and ours, but here, people didn't even know our real names.

I had to prove to Miss Shugart that our great-grandfather fought in the Civil War. When we got home, I pulled Abuelita's box from under the bed. She had sent some of her pictures and papers with us when we moved to Fort Steele. Maybe José del Carmel Cardenas's papers were here. Inside I found only marriage and death certificates, plus papers from the camposanto that showed Abuelita had paid for two plots. Abuelita must have kept her father's military papers in New Mexico, because I remembered her showing them to us once.

I put the box back under the bed and found some paper to write my abuelita a friendly letter.

*November 23, 1934*

*Dear Abuelita,*

*We are fine and hope you are well. I hope your artist friends are painting pictures of the mountains. They are beautiful covered with snow. We have snow here too. I think the weather is like New Mexico's, except there is more wind here. Sometimes we walk backward so the wind doesn't hit our faces.*

*At school Felícita is learning about the Civil War. Our teacher doesn't believe any Civil War battles were fought in New Mexico. If you can, please send me a paper to show her that your father fought in the war.*

*We are happy the money we are sending is helping you. We are having our matanza tomorrow.*

*Love,*

*Margarita*

All I had to do was wait for her to write back, and then I'd teach the teacher and the rest of the class a thing or two.

## CHAPTER 13

# San Lucas el Evangelista
## PATRON OF BUTCHERS

**Our matanza was** the next day. Even though it was later in the year than our other matanzas, at least it wasn't snowing, and the meat would stay fresh longer because it would freeze. Everyone in the family was up early. The toasty smell of tortillas perfumed the house. While Felícita flipped a tortilla on the comal, I snatched a warm one from the tall stack she had made. Then I left the house with the basket in one hand. Agustín Martínez was in the yard, adding logs to the fire pit. Steam rose from the water in Mamá's washtub, which sat on a grate above the fire. Alberto was digging a shallow garbage pit nearby. He wiped his brow on the sleeve of his coat.

"Buenos días le de Dios," I greeted Agustín, warming my hands near the fire. It had been so long since I greeted anyone outside our family this way. *This is a day where I can be myself*, I thought. I didn't have to try to say the right things every moment like I did around Caroline.

"Buenos días te de Dios," he replied. Then he pointed

to the basket and rubbed his hands. "Save me some huevos for my breakfast tomorrow. Ah, qué bueno—chile verde y huevos." He mixed Spanish and English when he spoke, like many of our gente.

I laughed. "I'll save you the biggest eggs." I looked around. "Where's the pig?"

"He's tied up behind the chicken coop. That son of a gun. I know you've been feeding him good, but he's still little."

"I think I'll have a look." I walked over to where Papá was sharpening his knife. An ax leaned against the shed. The hog cried like it knew what was going to happen. Poor little pig who had to die for us.

Papá ran his finger along the edge of the knife. "Well, hijita. We need to do this to feed dos familias." He spit on the whetting stone and rubbed the knife's edge against it. "You better get the eggs so Ernesto can take them to the store. He said he doesn't want to see the next part, where Agustín slaughters the pig."

Once Ernesto left for the store, Papá and Alberto moved a table with space between its planks near the garbage pit. All the parts we didn't want from the pig would be thrown into the pit. Mamá placed a white enameled pan below the table to catch the blood. Alberto led the pig near the table. With the heel of the ax, Agustín aimed at a spot between the pig's eyes. Then he swung it hard. The pig's legs buckled and it fell down. Papá and Alberto lifted the pink mass to the table, where Agustín jabbed his knife in the pig's throat. When the blood finished flowing into the enameled pan, Mamá took it into the house to keep the blood warm. Abuela would mix the blood with onions, garlic, fat, and herbs so we could make morcilla—blood sausage.

Papá ladled boiling hot water over the pig's skin so the hide would soften and the bristles would scrape off more easily. I picked up a bucket and walked to the water pump to refill the tub over the fire. As I pumped the handle, Ernesto ran into the yard, swinging the empty basket.

"I saw Caroline," he said. "She said she's coming over later. She has something she wants to show you, and it can't wait until Sunday."

"What is it?" What would be so important that Caroline would miss part of her church service?

Ernesto shrugged. "I don't know."

I picked up the basket. "Papá said they need you to get more wood."

"Is the pig dead?"

I nodded. "It's safe."

Later that morning, Esmeralda and Dolores came over

to help. They brought Tomás to play with Ernesto. It was my job to keep the water tub filled, which meant I got to stand by the fire and stay warm, unless I needed to get water from the pump. Once the scalding water softened the hide, the men butchered the pig. Even though this was a little pig, there was quite a bit of fat on him. Papá cut a big slab of it with bits of meat on the edges. Later, Mamá would cut the fat into cubes and cook it until it became crispy. My stomach growled when I thought about eating a bean-and-chicharrónes burrito with green chile.

At last, it was time for lunch. Caroline came into the yard as Papá and Agustín were cleaning up the butchering area. "Hi, Maggie. What are they doing, and what's that smell?" she asked, pinching her nose with one hand. In the other hand, she held a large envelope.

"They just finished butchering a pig for our matanza."

"Pig! You eat pig?" She didn't even wait for me to answer. "You're not supposed to eat pig. It says so in the Bible. You should be eating other things. Us Seventh-day Adventists never eat it."

I crossed my arms. "We *do* eat other things—like beans. Don't you remember when Joe called us beaners?"

"I never heard that." She laughed a nervous laugh and shook her curls.

Good. I had her squirming. She deserved it after what she said about Felícita.

"What I really came for was this." She handed me the large envelope.

I sat on the top porch step, lifted the flap, and pulled out a picture. It was Shirley Temple!

"Ohhh," I said, studying the large picture. Shirley Temple must have gone to a photographer's studio to take the photograph. You could see her from the waist up. Her hand was under her chin and she looked serious. Sausage-looking curls covered her head, and she wore a light-colored dress with dark lacing on the sleeves and down the front. At the bottom, it was signed, *It's Shirley wonderful having a friend like you. Love, Shirley Temple.*

"She even signed it in cursive writing!" I said.

"I doubt that she signed it," Caroline said. "She's as old as Ernie. Can he write in cursive?"

"Not yet," I said, and slipped the picture back into the envelope. "But she still sent a picture. Come in. I want to show everyone." I pointed to a nail on the porch wall. "You can hang your coat there."

Felícita was setting the table with Dolores's help. I showed them the picture.

"Qué linda," Dolores said, passing the picture on to Mamá and Dolores's mom.

"Yes, she's very pretty," Mamá said, making sure to speak in English for Caroline's sake.

When everyone had seen the picture, I reminded

Alberto, who was drying his hands, "You promised you would take us to the movies. Shirley Temple's in a new one."

Ernesto piped up, "I want to see it too, even if she is a girl." Everyone laughed.

"I promise," Alberto said.

Papá held a chair out for Caroline. "Please sit and share our meal," he said.

"Well, I just came to bring the picture, but maybe I could stay a while."

When everyone was seated, Papá blessed the food. "En el nombre del Padre, y del Hijo, y del Espíritu Santo." We all made the sign of the cross, except Caroline. Papá thanked God in Spanish for all our blessings, especially the meal and those who prepared it. When he finished the prayer, we all said, "Amen," except for Caroline. She cleared her throat.

Mamá passed the dishes around the table. Caroline turned to me and whispered, "You need to tell me what the foods are—in English."

"Would you like some fried potatoes?" I asked, holding the spoon over the bowl.

She nodded and I put some potatoes on her plate.

"How about some beans?"

Caroline took a serving.

Mamá passed a basket of tortillas around, and Caroline took two. She also took a helping of calabacitas because she could probably see that it was just corn, squash, and onions. Caroline passed the crispy chicharrónes on to me after I told her it was pork, but she did take some fresh green chile.

"Do you want me to show you how to make a burrito?" Ernesto asked her.

"Sure," she said.

"First you take a tortilla and put beans in the middle. Then you add green chile, onions, and some crispy chicharrónes from the pig, if you want. Now you roll it up like a cigarro," he said. Ernesto took a bite of his burrito. His eyes moved from side to side like the black cat clock and he wiggled his eyebrows.

Caroline smiled and made her own burrito with beans, onion, and green chile. She took a bite and swallowed. The next thing I knew she was fanning her mouth with her hand. She gulped some water and her eyes got bigger. She stood up. "My mouth!" she said, patting her lips.

"Margarita, get some milk from the icebox," Mamá said.

Caroline sucked in air, trying to cool her mouth. "No, I'm going," she said when she exhaled. She left the table, grabbed the envelope with the picture, and hurried to the door.

I followed her as she bounded down the porch stairs with her coat.

"Maggie, how could you?" she yelled.

"What?" I asked.

"You knew that green stuff was hot and you didn't even tell me."

"I told you it was chile!"

"That's right—I heard you say chilly! *Chilly* means something is cold, not burning hot! You're just trying to get even with me because I said I didn't believe your sister. I don't know why you're being so mean. The picture was mailed to my grandpa and I was going to share it with you. It's mine now!"

I stomped my foot. "Caroline, you're crazy! Since we've moved here, I've done everything to try to fit in with you, but you can't even remember that I'm from *New* Mexico, not Mexico! I went with you to your church—remember? But you couldn't even say *Amen* at our table, and I know we pray to the same God. We always have things your way because you're really bossy. That's why no one plays with you at school." I took a deep breath. "And that picture is mine! I spent more time thinking about and writing the letter than you spent mailing the envelope. *And* I paid for the stamp too! You're selfish."

Caroline was already by the chicken coop when she turned around. "Well, the picture was addressed to the store and Grandpa gave it to me once he opened it."

"Never mind then!" I shouted. "Keep it! I wasn't expecting a letter or a picture anyway. Maybe Shirley Temple will be your friend!"

She put her hands on her hips. "I *will* keep it! And you'll be sorry!"

I stomped up the steps. I *was* sorry. Sorry I used the store as the return address on the envelope. Sorry I'd ever tried to be friends with that selfish Caroline.

Felícita was clearing the table when I went into the kitchen. It was just as well. I wasn't hungry anymore. "I wrapped your burrito in wax paper," she said. "Do you want it now?"

"Maybe I'll eat it later, but thank you."

"How's Caroline?" Mamá asked.

"She's fine," I said.

"Good. But I hope we didn't scare her away from eating with us again."

I shrugged.

The Martínez family visited for a while after lunch and then went home with their share of the pork from the matanza. It had been a good matanza up until the argument with Caroline.

The rest of the day I had a heavy feeling in my gut as if I had eaten a big meal. Abuela always said a full belly equals a happy heart: "Panza llena, corazón contento." But my heart wasn't happy. It was wrong for Caroline to keep Shirley Temple's picture, but it was also wrong of me to shout at her. But then, she should listen to me sometimes. Friends shouldn't need to shout to be heard.

That evening before bedtime, I knelt in front of our home altar, crossed myself, and prayed.

*Bless me, Lord, for I have sinned. It's been a long time since I made a confession, but I need to make one tonight. I'm sorry I was mean to Caroline all because of a picture. I shouted at her, and I know that's not what friends do. Caroline needs me to be her friend. And I need her to be my friend. Please forgive me. Amen.*

I made an Act of Contrition, crossed myself again, and got in bed next to Abuela. If I had made my confession to a priest, he would have given me a penance. Instead, my mind gave me a penance that wouldn't let me sleep. It kept playing a movie of our fight earlier in the day.

Caroline needed me. Sometimes she was so bossy that I didn't want to be her friend. But I still liked her too. She was a hard worker like me, and I could tell she loved her family and they loved her. We both liked reading and learning, and she helped me practice English. Maybe I needed to give Caroline time to forget she was mad at me. Could I just avoid her for a while like Felícita said once? Then I wouldn't have the temptation to sin more and I could calm down too. Maybe then we could both say we were sorry.

## CHAPTER 14

# Santa Cecilia
## PATRONESS OF MUSIC

**Monday morning, I** let Ernesto deliver the eggs to Mr. Sims. Caroline usually went to her grandparents' house in the morning before she went to school, and I couldn't face her. Not yet.

Ernesto slid into his desk just as everyone got ready to say the Pledge. The desk in front of me remained empty, though. Where was Caroline?

After the Pledge, Miss Shugart made an announcement. "Students, the Christmas program is right around the corner. Because this is a short week due to Thanksgiving, I thought we'd get an early start learning our Christmas songs and poems for the pageant. As you're copying your spelling words, I'll meet with groups to assign parts."

I took out my Big Chief notebook and started copying the sixth-grade spelling words from the blackboard. This happened every week, and I would usually poke Caroline in the back and ask her what some of the words meant. I couldn't believe it, but I missed her today. I also had no idea what an *encyclopedia* was.

Out of the corner of my eye, I noticed Miss Shugart tap Ernesto on the shoulder. He followed her to the back of the room. Then she came over to my desk and asked me to join the two of them.

"I'm so pleased with the progress you've both made," Miss Shugart said to us. "Since you're doing so well, I'd like you both to recite 'A Visit from Saint Nicholas' at the program." She cocked her head. "Did you hear it at your old school?"

"No," we both said.

"I thought perhaps you hadn't, so I made you a copy. Take it home and practice it together."

"Miss Shugart," I said, "do you know where Caroline is?"

"Oh, yes, her grandfather sent me a note. Her father is home from the railroad today, so she's spending time with him."

I nodded. When I sat down at my desk, I read through the poem. What kind of word was 'Twas? Who was Saint Nicholas? I had never heard of him or seen a statue of him. Was a sugar plum a prune? What was he putting in the stockings? I liked the rhymes all the way through the long poem. I put it in my notebook next to my spelling list.

After she finished meeting with everyone, Miss Shugart clapped her hands for attention. "I'm sure most of you remember the tunes to these Christmas songs, but let's go over them to be sure we all know the words." Then she blew a note on her pitch pipe. "We'll start with a fun one—'Jingle Bells.'"

I didn't know the song, but Miss Shugart had the class sing it a couple of times. Pretty soon, I learned most of the words and could join in singing the chorus. Ernesto, Felícita, and Dolores seemed to enjoy the singing too.

"Raise your hand if you listened to Eddie Cantor's show last night," Miss Shugart said. About half the kids in the school raised their hands. We didn't have a radio, but I knew it was Caroline's favorite show. She never missed it. "On Sunday evening, I heard a new song called 'Santa Claus Is Coming to Town.' Lucky for me, they played it quite a few times, so I was able to write down the words. Let me sing it first. Then I'll say a phrase and you can echo me."

We echoed Miss Shugart until we could sing the whole song by ourselves. The music was lively—the kind that made you want to tap your toes. I had so much fun singing that I even forgot about my problems with Caroline.

Before I knew it, school was over for the day and it was time to go home. I walked with Ernesto and Tomás. Felícita walked ahead of us with Dolores. They were laughing about something while I had to listen to Ernesto tell his goofy jokes for the hundredth time.

I hummed the tune we learned in school all the way home, swinging Ernesto's hand to the beat. As we crossed the railroad tracks, he asked, "Who's Santa Claus?"

"I don't know. One of the saints, I guess, like Santa María or Santa Teresa. We can ask Abuela."

"Yeah, she knows all the saints."

When we got home, I started my after-school chores. I gathered some of the logs stacked in the woodshed and took them to the kitchen. The hungry black stove swallowed one log.

"Supper's almost ready," Mamá said. "Go get your abuela."

I took a lit lantern and tiptoed into the bedroom Felícita and I shared with Abuela. She was praying the rosary, and her rocking chair kept the beat as she prayed. I sat down on the squeaky bed and tried not to fidget. When she said, "Amen," I touched her arm.

"Buenas noches," I greeted Abuela.

Her wrinkled hands found my forehead, where she made the sign of the cross. "Buenas noches, Margarita."

"Do you know Santa Claus?" I asked, gently draping her rosary beads over her beloved gold-painted statue of the Virgin Mary.

"Is she a Wyoming saint?" Abuela asked.

"I don't know. I heard the name in school. How about Saint Nicholas?"

She shook her head and motioned for me to help her up. We went arm in arm to the kitchen for supper. If Abuela didn't know Santa Claus or Saint Nicholas, maybe they were saints just for Wyoming children and not for New Mexican children.

After supper, Ernesto and I practiced "A Visit from Saint Nicholas." I would say one phrase, then Ernesto would repeat it. I wondered how a saint could fit down our skinny chimney. Even after reading the poem a couple of times, I couldn't think what this saint might be invoked for. There were also some words I had trouble pronouncing and understanding. I decided to ask Miss Shugart for help tomorrow. I'd also ask her about Santa Claus and Saint Nicholas.

# CHAPTER 15

## San Cayetano

### PATRON OF THE UNEMPLOYED, JOB SEEKERS, AND GOOD FORTUNE

**The next morning,** Mr. Sims was working behind the counter when Ernesto and I came in with the eggs. He put both hands on the counter and winked at Ernesto. "Are you practicing telling time like I taught you?" he asked. Ernesto nodded. "Well, go ahead and practice some more," Mr. Sims said.

Ernesto went across the room to see that crazy cat clock. Mr. Sims flipped the ledger pages until he got to Papá's name. He counted the eggs, wrote down some numbers, then pushed his glasses up on his nose and shut the ledger. "You've earned six dollars and sixty cents—the bill for that lantern's almost paid up. Maybe next time."

I smiled.

"I know your garden is out of commission now, but people enjoyed having the fresh foods. Speaking of fresh foods, you might notice that the tor . . . tor-tillas you bring are all sold out. Even the missus bought some."

"That's good," I said. "I'll ask Mamá when we can make more."

He chuckled. "You better hurry on to school. I suspect Caroline will be late today. Her dad's still on his layover. But after school, she'll be here for sure. She knows we're expecting a shipment."

I ran all the way to school, lifting my face to the wind. If I had shouted, the wind could have carried my words like Mr. Sims's telephone. Everyone could have heard the good news. People in town liked our vegetables, eggs, and tortillas—even Mrs. Sims. And now the bill for the lantern was almost paid. Soon we'd be able to send more money to help Abuelita Cruzita.

Miss Shugart had a custom of inviting students inside before school started to help her get ready for the day. Ernesto wanted to play in the schoolyard, so he didn't come in with me. I stoked the fire in the potbellied stove and put graded papers on students' desks.

"Miss Shugart," I said as she wrote sentences on the blackboard, "could you help me with 'A Visit from Saint Nicholas'? My brother and I don't know what all the words in the poem mean."

"Dear, I know Caroline would love to help you. She

recited the poem last year. I'll give you time to work together today."

"But ... but ... ," I said, as Miss Shugart handed me the school bell. I wanted to avoid Caroline for a few more days.

"Please go outside and let everyone know school is starting," Miss Shugart said.

I stood in the door and rang the bell. When Felícita walked by me, I pulled her aside and whispered the good news Mr. Sims told me. She squeezed my hand.

Caroline came in late, like her grandfather had said. She didn't look at me.

The morning went by as fast as the "coursers" that flew in the poem, whatever those were. Just before lunch, Dolores and Tomás came into the classroom. They had been gone all morning. Dolores handed Miss Shugart a note. Tomás sat down, but Miss Shugart kept talking to Dolores, who wiped her eyes with a handkerchief.

I caught Felícita's eye and mouthed, "What's wrong?" She shrugged.

Finally, it was lunchtime, and I took my lunch bucket and sat with Felícita and Dolores. "What's the matter?" Felícita asked as she rubbed Dolores's back.

"We have to leave," Dolores said. "We're going back."

"What do you mean, you're going back?" I asked.

"We're going back to New Mexico." Dolores blew her

nose in her wadded-up handkerchief. "Papá lost his job."

"What!" Felícita jumped up. "Why?"

Dolores fidgeted with her hands as if she was praying the rosary. "A railroad investigator came to the house this morning. He said someone told him Papá had another job as a *butcher*. Someone saw him cutting up the pig this weekend. The man said the railroad has rules about working two jobs, and then he fired Papá." Her shoulders shook and she buried her face in her hands. Felícita handed Dolores a fresh handkerchief.

"That's crazy!" I said. "All he did was *help* our papá. Who would even know your papá butchered the pig?"

"I don't know," Dolores said, wiping her eyes.

Suddenly, it came to me. My mouth went dry and I couldn't speak. Caroline! She saw Agustín and Papá after they cut up the pig by the chicken coop. And if this story got Agustín fired, it could get Papá and Alberto fired next. They might have already lost their jobs.

I got up and paced around the schoolyard. Is this what Caroline meant when she told me I'd be sorry? No, even she wouldn't try to get Papá fired. Maybe she told people about our matanza and someone misunderstood what she said. But if Papá and Alberto were out of work, what would we do? The eggs and tortillas didn't bring us much money. Everything could collapse around us. I had to find out if Caroline had said anything.

Miss Shugart rang the bell, and we all lined up and went into the classroom. Once we were at our desks, she said, "Students, we're going to partner up to practice for the program. Ernie, I want you to go with your sister and Caroline." She looked at me and Caroline. "I know Ernie will do fine with both of you helping him."

"Yes, Miss Shugart," I said dully. "Ernesto, get the papers and sit by the stove."

Caroline walked over to the stove too. "Miss Shugart said she gave you a poem yesterday. What are you going to read?" Her voice sounded like she had forgotten everything that had happened between us and she didn't know about Dolores's family.

I folded my arms. "'A Visit from Saint Nicholas.'"

"Oh, that one," she said, with a toss of her head. "I memorized it last year. It's so easy. I can help you with it."

"I *know* you learned it last year," I said. What I really wanted to say was *Did you tell the railroad men Dolores's dad had a second job?* But I couldn't say anything because we were in school.

"Explain it to us," Ernesto said. "We don't know who Santa Claus is and neither does our abuela."

Caroline leaned in. "You never heard of Santa Claus? Where have you been all your lives?"

"You know where we've been," I said. "New Mexico."

She motioned for us to come closer as if she was going

to tell us a secret. She spoke in a low voice. "Santa Claus brings gifts to well-behaved children on Christmas Eve. Kids usually write him a letter asking for a special gift. So if you're good from now until Christmas, he'll bring you what you want."

Ernesto cocked his head. "What? Isn't Santa Claus a woman?"

Caroline shook her head. "Don't be silly. Santa Claus is a little fat man."

"But Saint Nicholas is a man saint, right?" Ernesto added.

"Yes, but Saint Nicholas is the same person as Santa Claus. Saint Nicholas was what people called him a long time ago in Holland, I think."

"Hmmm. Only women saints are Santas for us," Ernesto said.

I was too upset and worried to care about the difference between Santa Claus and Saint Nicholas. "Miss Shugart said we need to practice the poem. So let's do it."

Ernesto read the poem out loud, and Caroline explained what some of the words meant. *Coursers* were running animals—in this poem, reindeer, which were a kind of deer in the far north. Ernesto asked Caroline what Saint Nicholas was putting in the stockings. She surprised us with her answer—toys. While we were reading the poem for the third time, Miss Shugart interrupted. "Class, it's time for everyone to go back to their seats and get ready to go home."

Ernesto and I picked up our papers. Caroline said, "Hey, do you both want to come to the store after school? Grandpa said there should be toys in the shipment today. Maybe you'll see something you want. Then we could write Santa Claus a letter and ask him for presents."

"I can't ask him. I don't know him," Ernesto said.

"Well, he knows you. He knows everything."

"How does he know if you've been nice like the song says?" Ernesto asked.

"He's got some special powers, and I think parents tell him things," Caroline said. "You'll meet him at the school Christmas program. He always comes—and with presents."

My arms were still crossed. He never came to our old school. The only presents we got were gifts of food when we went to houses in the village for Mis Crismes. Besides, I had never heard of a saint who was still alive.

Caroline chewed on her bottom lip and looked at Ernesto and then at me. "Don't you want to come to the store?"

Ernesto shook his head. "Not me. I want to go skating with Sam. But I'll tell Mamá that Margarita went with you."

I fixed my eyes on Ernesto. "I'm supposed to help you with the poem."

"No, go ahead. Mamá will help me," he said. "Tell Mr. Sims hello for me."

Ernesto didn't understand. I didn't want to go to the store and pretend everything was hunky-dory, as Caroline liked to say. But if Caroline was telling lies because she was mad at me, I had to be nice to her. If Papá lost his job, it would be my fault.

I was glad it was cold outside so I could wrap my scarf around my mouth. We walked to the store in silence until Caroline spoke up.

"I'm sorry for the way I acted on Saturday, Maggie. I told Daddy what I said about your sister. I even told him how I held my nose when you told me your family killed a pig. He said that was rude and I wasn't being a very good friend. And you were right. The picture belongs to you. That was really selfish of me."

This was my best friend speaking. At that moment, Caroline's apology meant more to me than any picture. "No. Go ahead and keep it."

"That would just prove I'm spoiled."

I smiled. "You're a little spoiled. But you can't help it if you don't have sisters and brothers."

She blew out her breath like a locomotive when it arrived at the station. "I also told Daddy about your hot chile. He told me about the time your brother gave him a tortilla with green chile in it. He said it burned his mouth too at first, but the next bite wasn't so hot. In fact, he said he even trades his liverwurst sandwiches for your brother's bur . . . burritos now. He and Grandpa reminded me that your family has worked hard to learn our ways, and the least we can do is put ourselves in your shoes and learn more about your ways." She bit her lip. "Daddy told me about the Martínez family. I know how much you'll miss your friends. I know I'd miss you if you moved back to Mexico." She looked down at her shoes. "I'm really sorry for everything. Can we be friends again?"

I nodded. From the way she was talking, I could tell Caroline didn't tell anyone but her dad about the butchering. "I'm sorry too, Caroline. I never should have shouted at you and said those mean things." I took a deep breath. "But you just basically said I'm from old Mexico. I do want you to remember that I'm a proud New Mexican from the state of New Mexico, just like you're a proud Wyomingite. And even though we speak Spanish and eat foods like they do in Mexico, we're Americans just like everyone here in Fort Steele."

She nodded back to me. "I can do that." A smirk appeared on her face, and she tapped her head with her finger. "Remember before when I said you're *New* Mexican because you're not old? I need to remember that to keep it straight."

I rolled my eyes and took her hand. "And I don't think you want to put yourself in my shoes. They're smaller than yours."

She smiled. "What if we shared the picture . . . like sisters do?" she asked.

I smiled back. "Maybe that would work."

We went inside the store. Mr. Sims was busy unpacking some big boxes. "Well, if it isn't the two prettiest and smartest ladies in town," he said, wiping his brow.

Caroline went behind the counter and hung up her coat. "Oh, Grandpa, you're just saying that."

Mr. Sims laughed, his eyes landing on me. "Well, your friend Margarita speaks two languages, doesn't she? I think that makes her pretty smart." He waved at the back of the store. "I think you girls might be interested in some of the boxes that came in today," he said.

"We'll help you open them," Caroline said.

Mr. Sims glanced over his glasses at her. "Caroline, friends don't tell friends what to do." Then he asked me, "Do you want to help?"

"I'll stay a little while," I said as I took off my coat.

Caroline held out her hand. "I'll hang that up for you."

We opened a box from Montgomery Ward's and uncovered a shiny new washing machine. Another box had more long, colorful boxes inside. They had a picture of a little man dressed in a black suit and a tall black hat. He stood next to a simple picture of a train engine. Letters on the cover spelled MONOPOLY.

Caroline shrieked. "Maggie, look! A new one. They

made a new one!" She held up a box with a new Shirley Temple doll inside. "We have to write to Santa Claus and ask him to bring us Shirley Temple dolls for Christmas."

The doll was beautiful. Maybe I could ask Santa Claus for one. It would look pretty sitting on the dresser in our room at home, but it cost two dollars and ninety-nine cents. Caroline stood the doll on top of the toy shelf while I finished unpacking the rest of the box. From the bottom I pulled out a thin book with Shirley Temple's picture on the cover. Each page had clothes to cut out with little white tabs on them. I even recognized some of the outfits from *Little Miss Marker*. "Look at her pretty clothes," I said.

Caroline turned up her nose at the book. "Those are paper dolls. We want real dolls." She pushed the empty box aside and dusted off her dress. "I guess that's the end of the toys for today. We could start writing our letters to Santa Claus now."

"Maybe tomorrow, girls," Mr. Sims said. "Caroline, I told your grandma you'd help her in the kitchen after we unpacked this shipment. She's planning three different kinds of pies for Thanksgiving."

"I can't stay any later anyway," I said. "My mother is waiting for me."

Caroline handed me my coat and walked me to the door. "Well, I hope your family has a happy Thanksgiving. And maybe I'll see you this weekend."

"Sure," I said. "See you."

"Wait. I almost forgot." She picked up a big envelope behind the counter and handed it to me. "Here, it's your turn to have Shirley Temple at your house."

I opened the envelope and took out the picture of Shirley. "Thanks, but like I said, you don't have to do this."

"Remember? I said we could share it like sisters do." Caroline pointed to the signature on the picture. "Or at least it could be like the writing says, 'It's Shirley wonderful having a friend like you.'"

I put the picture back in the envelope. "It surely is! Bye for now."

*What a good start to Thanksgiving*, I thought as I walked home. I didn't know why I ever thought Caroline told on Agustín. She was sorry the Martínezes were leaving. She wouldn't tell on Papá, either, because then we'd be gone too.

But . . . who did tell on them?

The minute I got home, I put the signed picture next to the pretty blue sugar bowl with Shirley Temple's picture.

## CHAPTER 16

# Santa Brígida
## PATRONESS OF FUGITIVES

**On Wednesday, I** took eight eggs to the Simses' store. I had been working for this day since I broke the lantern. Mr. Sims opened his ledger book. "You are paid in full. Congratulations." Then we shook hands.

Thanksgiving vacation gave us a long weekend. We had a good dinner because we had just killed a pig at our matanza. I was thankful that our family was all together. Last year Papá and Alberto were the only ones in Wyoming. After we said grace, Papá invited each of us to close our eyes and add something to our prayer. Abuela Rufina thanked God for familia. Mamá gave thanks for Papá's and Alberto's jobs. Felícita added being grateful for our good health. When I gave thanks that the lantern I broke was paid for, I opened my eyes and saw that everyone was smiling. Ernesto was grateful that the egg money was now going to Abuelita for the land. Papá gave thanks for the help the Martínezes gave us with the matanza and for all of us being together. Alberto ended the prayer asking for a safe journey for the Martínez family, who had already left for New Mexico.

"I hope Agustín finds a job back home," I said.

"He has one already," Papá said as he passed the green chile to Felícita.

"Doing what?" she asked.

"Working the farm and herding their sheep. He's in charge now that his papá died."

Felícita and I looked at each other. Was that why the family left? What about his getting fired?

Papá put some red chile gravy on top of his mashed potatoes. "I wish he could have stayed here. It was easier to go to the back room at the store with the other railroaders when he was with me. But he was worried about a visa he said we needed." He shook his head. "He was always afraid someone would try to deport him to Old Mexico. I told him we didn't have to worry because we were both born in the United States."

Felícita scowled. "Our family didn't cross the border. The border crossed us."

We all laughed and Papá wiped his eyes. "That's right. You should have told my compadre this. First our land was called New Spain or Nueva Mexico. When Mexico won its independence from Spain, our land became Mexican land. In the Mexican-American War, Mexico lost its land to the United States, so then it got an English name—New

Mexico." He put three fingers in the air. "Three borders! But I think Agustín is happy to be home again, even if Esmeralda and the kids wanted to stay here."

I put my fork down. "I've never seen you in the back room when I've been at the store with Caroline."

He looked at Alberto. "We've both been there. It's important to go sometimes, to try to make friends with the other railroaders. I even met your friend's papá—the engineer. He told me he was going to put in a good word for us with Mr. Maroni."

"Her papá is really nice," I said. "I'll bet he can help you. The Simses are our friends."

"Sí," Abuela said, patting my hand. "Pero, al amigo y al caballo, no cansarlos."

I squeezed my abuela's hand back. "Papá would never take advantage of friends."

As we cleared the table, Ernesto piped up, "Do you want to hear the Christmas poem me and Margarita are going to say at the program?"

"You mean, Margarita and I," Papá said.

Ernesto's eyes got really big. "I didn't know you were going to say the poem, Papá."

Papá laughed. "I'm not." He ruffled Ernesto's hair. "First we clean up, then we'll hear your poem."

After the last dish had been put away, everyone sat down in the parlor. I held the paper Miss Shugart gave us so Ernesto and I could read "A Visit from Saint Nicholas" together.

After we finished, everyone clapped. "When's your program?" Alberto asked.

"I'll check the calendar. I know how to use it," Ernesto said. He ran into the kitchen and came back with the calendar. His finger ran across next month's days. "December nineteenth is a Wednesday. Santa Claus is coming to the program that night."

Alberto slapped his leg. "I want to meet this Santa Claus. I hear he gives presents."

"He does, and he's a *live* saint," Ernesto said. "But you need to write him a letter first. He even has a special mailbox at the Sims store."

Papá laughed. "Unless there's a derailment or some other problem, we should be able to get cleaned up in time to see the program and this Santa Claus."

Ernesto tugged on Papá's arm. "We're going to sing songs too."

"Will you be singing songs to la Virgen?" Mamá flicked a wisp of hair from her eyes. "Her feast day is on the twelfth."

"No," I said. "All the songs are in English. I don't think anyone knows about the Virgin's feast day here. But that reminds me. . . ." I looked at the calendar and counted nine days back from December twenty-fourth. "Las Posadas starts on December fifteenth. That's a Saturday. Could we maybe celebrate the first night?"

Papá pulled out his little work calendar from his plaid flannel shirt. He scratched his head. "I don't know. We'll be in the dead of winter then. Last winter, bearings froze on the trains and even the rails got brittle and snapped. We could be working twelve-hour shifts. We'll see, and we'll see about your school program."

I loved Las Posadas, but how could we reenact the Holy Family's trip to Bethlehem with the neighbors we had? They didn't know the Spanish songs or our traditions. And would they even want to play the pilgrims asking for lodging, or the innkeepers who keep refusing to let the people in? My heart ached for the family and friends we left in our little village.

Ernesto was still looking at the calendar. "We could celebrate Las Posadas Monday night because we don't have school Tuesday morning."

"One of those nights might work," Papá said.

"We could decorate with a few farolitos," I said. "I saw some paper sacks and candles in the porch. What do you think?"

"I suppose we could try," Papá said. "We could make a luminaria too—at least for one night. There should be enough wood for one bonfire."

"I'll put the days on the calendar," Ernesto said as he searched for a pencil.

Mamá untied her apron and folded it. She laughed. "I should just sleep in my apron."

"Why?" Ernesto asked.

She wiggled her finger at him. "Because I'll be wearing this almost every day if I'm going to make biscochitos, empanaditas, and tamales in time for Las Posadas and Christmas."

"We'll help you, Mamá," Felícita and I said almost at the same time.

"First we need to dig up all the root vegetables and get them ready for winter," Mamá said. "Then we can start making the empanaditas and biscochitos. It should be cold enough in the porch to keep some foods frozen."

★ ★ ★

We didn't have any school on Friday. Miss Shugart had said it was part of our Thanksgiving vacation. But it was no vacation digging up the beets, potatoes, and carrots that weekend. Mamá had us clean the vegetables and take them down to the cellar to store for the winter in big bins filled with sand. The cellar already held cabbages, wrapped in newspaper, waiting for Mamá to pickle them. There were also jars of pickled beets, a gunny sack full of beans, and pork wrapped in butcher paper. By the end of the first week of December, we were as ready for winter as the prairie dogs that burrowed underground.

On the eighth day of December, after I took Abuela to the outhouse, she linked her arm in mine as we went to the kitchen.

"Is your mamá making bread?" she asked, sniffing the air.

"No, Abuela, empanadita dough," I said.

The holiday smells from the kitchen were as welcoming as the room itself. The scent of licorice floated from the anise seeds that Felícita mixed into the biscochito dough. A new flour sack covered the rising dough for the empanaditas in a bowl on the stove. Mamá stood at the table, mixing ground cloves into the shredded pork. She added sugar, raisins, and chopped apples into the mixture. I couldn't wait to taste the little turnovers. Mamá wiped her hands on her apron, sat Abuela down at the table, and wrapped Abuela's hands around a cup of coffee, adding a splash of evaporated milk.

"What do you think Ernesto would like for Christmas?" I asked.

"I'm sure he'll be happy with the luminarias and farolitos," Mamá said.

"I know, but I want to ask Santa Claus to bring something special for him." I planned to write my letter to Santa Claus soon.

Mamá tipped the canister of flour and looked at me. "We're getting low. When the store opens after sundown,

I want you to go to the store and buy more. And see how much their applesauce costs. If it's too much, I'll just use the one wrinkled apple we have left." She picked up her rolling pin and dusted the table with the last of the flour. "Don't stay too long. We'll need your help here."

I found Caroline standing by the counter when I came in the store. After her grandfather counted our eggs and wrote the total in the ledger, she put them in the Frigidaire and closed the door. "Say, can you stay awhile so we can write to Santa Claus?"

"Well . . . I can't stay very long. We're planning a celebration."

Caroline wrinkled her forehead. "Thanksgiving is over, and it's not time for Christmas yet. What are you celebrating?"

"Las Posadas."

"What's that?"

"It's the time before Christmas when we remember the journey Joseph and Mary took to Bethlehem, and how they had to find a place for Mary to have the Christ child. *Posadas* means lodging. The celebration lasts nine days because it stands for the nine months Mary carried Christ before he was born."

"It must be a big celebration if it lasts nine days."

"Well, we're just going to celebrate one night."

"How do you celebrate?"

"It's kind of like a play. We sing a special song, and we burn luminarias to light the way for the Holy Family to find a place to stay in Bethlehem."

"Lum-in-ar-ee-as?" Caroline stumbled over the word.

"They're little bonfires. So I have to gather wood and help with the cooking until then."

"Maybe I could come over and help you . . . if you want me to," she said.

It surprised me that she asked me instead of telling me what she wanted to do. "I'd like that," I said. "I'll let you know when you can help."

Caroline smiled. "Okay, but first things first." Her usual bossy voice returned. She hung my coat on a hook and tapped the side of the counter. "Let's write to Santa Claus. I've got the paper and pens right here. It won't take long because you're such a good writer. Say, do you know which Shirley Temple doll you want?"

"No."

"Well, I do. I want the new one on the shelf. I already have the older one."

We sat down at the table behind the counter. In my very best penmanship I wrote,

December 8, 1934

Dear Santa Claus,

How are you? We are fine. We are getting ready
for Christmas. Do you like biscochitos? Felícita and I are
making some today. They are so crispy and good. Later
we are going to make empanaditas too. They are little
turnovers filled with sweet meat.

My little brother, Ernesto, would like any toy you
bring him. I would like a Shirley Temple doll or even
Shirley Temple paper dolls. If you don't have any of those
left, a picture of Shirley Temple would be the next thing
I'd like. Then I could give it to my friend and we would
each have our own.

Feliz Navidad to you and your family.

Sincerely yours,

Margarita Sandoval


Caroline peeked at my letter from her side of the table as
she blew the ink dry on hers. "Yours is so neat. I made so
many mistakes on mine."

Mr. Sims walked out to the counter from the back room.
"Well, well, what do we have here? It looks like two little
ladies just finished writing to Santa Claus. Now, be sure to
drop the letters in the North Pole mailbox over there." He
pointed to the new mailbox by the potbellied stove on the
other side of the store. "You don't need stamps."

We folded our holiday letters the way Miss Shugart taught us, and I put mine in the envelope Caroline handed me. We walked across the room to where the Kit-Cat Klock ticked. I had always called it a cat clock until Caroline and I unpacked some new ones and I saw the correct name.

"Excuse us," Caroline said to the two men sitting by the stove. They were drinking coffee, smoking cigarettes, and reading the newspaper. I could tell they worked for the railroad by their hats and overalls. "You first." She poked me in the ribs and pointed to the special mailbox.

I dropped my envelope in the slot and then Caroline dropped hers in. We walked back to the counter. The men's eyes were like the Kit-Cat Klock. They seemed to follow my every move.

"I have to get a few things and check on some prices for Mamá before I go." It was cold in the store, so I put my coat on.

"Go ahead, I'll just tidy the counter up a bit," Caroline said.

The canned foods were on one side of a tall shelf by the potbellied stove. The shelf separated the store from the room where the railroaders sat. As I reached for the applesauce, I heard a slurping sound, then the thud of a coffee cup hitting the table.

"That girl in the store. Ain't she one of those Mexican kids?"

"Yeah," the other voice growled.

"That other Mexican—Martínez. What's the story about him?"

I stopped moving and stood as quietly as I could. What did these men know about Agustín?

"All I knows is he hightailed it back to Mexico where he came from," the gruff voice replied, then he laughed. "After a little tip from yours truly."

"You caught him workin' off the clock? I didn't know you had such eagle eyes."

"I didn't see nothin', but I keep my ears open. That little beaner kid that hangs around this crazy clock was talking to old man Sims. He told Sims that Martínez was a butcher. You know the railroad's rules about having two jobs, so I told Maroni. Next thing you know—adiós, Martínez. He didn't even fight it."

Oh no. They were talking about Ernesto and Agustín. My heart pounded loud enough for the men to hear. Both of them laughed, and one blew his nose. I heard more coffee slurping.

The man with the gruff voice said, "I can't believe the railroad hired that kid's greaser father instead of my nephew. That's just not right. And after all the good work I did for them, the railroad owes me. We don't need their kind here. That whole family should go back—back to Mexico like the other ones."

The other man said, "Aaaaaamen," making it sound almost as long as a death sentence. "Well, I better head on out to the train. It's almost time for my run. Try to stay awake on your post, Sleepy."

*That Sleepy wants Papá fired too!* I waited until I heard the door open and close. *Please help me not get noticed*, I prayed. I tiptoed so the wooden floors wouldn't squeak. When I opened the door slowly, the bell barely tinkled. I ran to the tracks. A train passed by—an angry train, blowing steam. Like those men. I kept running.

My thoughts raced as fast as my feet. Ernesto told Mr. Sims that Agustín was the butcher for our matanza. Sleepy overheard him, and he got it all wrong. He told Mr. Maroni the wrong information. My heart felt like it was pierced by arrows, just like San Sebastián. I wiped away tears. Could Papá and Alberto lose their jobs next? What could I do to help protect them?

When our yard was in sight, I slowed down. My legs felt as heavy as the freight on the train as I dragged myself up the steps. I swallowed hard. In the kitchen, Mamá was punching down some risen dough. Ernesto had flour on his face like face powder.

"You sure were gone a long time," said Felícita. "Where's the flour?"

I bit my lip. "I forgot it."

Felícita slapped some biscochito dough to the kitchen

table. "Well, I hope there's enough flour for the next batch." She pointed to the sugar in a bowl. "Hurry up! Add the cinnamon to the sugar before the dough dries up."

There were circles of cookie dough already cut out, and the scraps were waiting to be rolled back together. I tied an apron on and climbed the step stool to reach the can of cinnamon sticks, but I fumbled and the can fell from the shelf, spilling the sticks. I dusted them off and grabbed a grater from the large crock on the counter.

Grating the cinnamon stick back and forth over the bowl of sugar gave me a chance to think. Maybe Santa Claus could help us. But I had already asked him for a doll. Why did I do that? I should have asked him for something important for everyone in the family—like helping Alberto and Papá keep their jobs. Familia should always come first. I dipped the cookie dough circles into the cinnamon-sugar mixture and placed them on the baking sheet.

Mamá opened the oven door for me, and I slipped the pan inside. "Do you know Santa Claus?" I asked her.

She used the back of her hand to push away some stray hairs that had escaped from her bun. "No, I don't know of that saint except from the song Ernesto sings. Why do you ask?"

"I thought maybe you could ask him something."

Felícita rolled her eyes. "How would she know him? You know we never heard of Santa Claus in New Mexico.

Besides that, I've never heard of a living saint."

My body drooped like a rag doll and tears flooded my eyes. "Well, we live in Wyoming now. Someone should know him."

Mamá lifted my chin and wiped my tears with her apron. Abuela reached out to me. I went into her warm hug. She whispered, "Al que se ayuda, Dios le ayuda."

Mamá gave her full attention to the empanadita dough. She squeezed it into doorknob-sized balls, dusted flour onto her rolling pin, and rolled out one circle. She dropped a scoop of sweet meat in the center and folded it into a bulging turnover. As I helped her pinch the edges to bind the sweetness inside, I tucked in my silent Christmas prayer for Papá and Alberto to keep their jobs.

But Abuela was right. I needed to do something before God would answer my prayer. So, after we cleaned up the baking supplies and cleared the table, I sat down and wrote Santa Claus another letter. He just had to get the letter before he came to the Christmas pageant.

*December 8, 1934*
*Dear Santa Claus,*

*I know I wrote you a letter earlier, but this is what I really want for Christmas. I want Papá and Alberto to be safe and keep their jobs. They take care of us and send money to help our grandmother in New Mexico* with our land. They're hard workers, and that's why the railroad needs them. Even though we miss New Mexico, our family likes our new town and we want to stay. We hope the people here will like us too.

Your friend,
Margarita Sandoval

## CHAPTER 17

# Santiago el Mayor
## PATRON OF SPAIN
## AND THE CHRISTIAN ARMY

**On Monday morning,** Ernesto and I each ate an empanadita with some Ovaltine for breakfast. Then he took the eggs to the store. I put my letter to Santa Claus in my Big Chief notebook and went to school bright and early to help Miss Shugart get things ready.

When everyone filed in the schoolroom, Caroline pulled me over. "You can tell Christmas is coming. We were swamped Saturday evening! But I didn't see you after you checked on whatever it was for your mother. I thought maybe you were going to tell me more about your special celebration."

"Something came up, and I needed to leave. You can help later. We have time."

"Good. Because your holiday sounds like fun. Can you come to the store after school?" she asked.

I was all ready to give her an excuse why I wouldn't be there today either. But that would make me exactly what Ernesto called people who were scared—a fraidycat.

Sure, those men hurt my pride and my feelings, but they couldn't do anything to me. If the railroaders were in the store, I might even learn something that could help Papá and Alberto, and I could mail my second letter to Santa Claus. Also, it wasn't Caroline's fault how I felt, and here she was, excited to help with our Posadas.

I lifted my head and smiled. "Sure. I'll go with you."

After school, Caroline and I hung our coats on the hooks behind the store counter. There were quite a few customers, so she took her place by the cash register while I grabbed a broom. I thought I'd start in the back room so I could listen to the railroaders, but there was no one there. I slipped my letter in the special mailbox, then started sweeping near where Mr. Sims was talking to a customer.

"Looks like business is good," the man said.

Mr. Sims laughed. "That's for sure. The women in this town have the Christmas spirit! Which reminds me, I need to get over to the pump house and take some measurements. We're giving the railroaders a surprise."

The pump house. Lots of railroaders went to the pump house to take showers. Even Papá and Alberto went there after their work shifts. I wondered what it was like.

When the man left, I stopped sweeping and went up to Mr. Sims. "Excuse me, Mr. Sims. Caroline and I can get those measurements at the pump house for you if you'd like."

Mr. Sims smiled. "That would help me out a lot. Thank you. You just need to measure the little room right inside the door. I'll get the tape measure."

While he went in the back room, I told Caroline what her grandfather wanted us to do. She was as curious to see inside the pump house as I was. Women and children usually never went there. We took our baths in tin tubs at home.

We walked toward the river carrying the tape measure, a pencil, and paper. It was windy and cold, and our feet made imprints in the crusty snow. When we arrived at the pump house, we saw railroaders covered in soot and dirt. They were heading inside to shower, carrying towels and bulging pillowcases probably filled with their clean clothes. I recognized the man ahead of us by the door. Alberto had pointed him out as one of the conductors who worked on the train. His wife bought our tortillas. "Sure have some dirty clothes today," the conductor said to another man as he held the door open for us. "My wife wonders if I'm working on an oil rig."

The other man laughed. "Ain't that the truth. The U.P. should do something about all that oil on the tracks. I saw a little spill today by the bridge. I think it's coming from some freight trains, but can't put my finger on it."

Both men stopped in the little room. The conductor said, "You girls shouldn't go beyond this space. The shower for railroaders is in the next room."

I nodded. "We're just here to measure *this* room and then we'll leave."

He tugged on one of Caroline's long curls. "Be sure and tell your daddy I'm looking forward to being his conductor this week. I don't need to help him as much as I help the other engineers. He's a good man with the train."

Caroline blushed. "Thank you, Mr. Dugan."

The men headed for the showers. I put the pencil behind my ear as I positioned the tape measure against the wall.

"Daddy likes to work with Mr. Dugan too," Caroline told me. "Sometimes the other conductors don't want to go outside in bad weather and check on the trains. They want to stay inside with the engineers and keep warm, but that's not their job."

I nodded and pulled the pencil from behind my ear. "I'll measure if you want to write down the numbers."

"Sure. That'll work," she said as she took the pencil. "I wonder what Grandpa wants the measurements for. Did he tell you?"

"No." We worked quickly, and when we were done, I stood up and wiped the grit from my knees. "It will be dark soon. I need to get home." I wanted to tell Papá and Alberto everything I had heard.

I waved to Caroline until I saw that she was on the other side of the tracks. Then I walked carefully up the slippery embankment, as close to the bridge as I could get, to see the oil spill. There was some oil and a bit of coal on the dry weeds near the tracks, close to the bridge.

When I got home, Papá was coming down the steps. He carried his lantern and had his work clothes on.

"Buenas noches, Papá. Another shift tonight?"

"Yes, our crew needs to break some ice."

"I hope you got a little rest."

He nodded. "I didn't even hear the train whistles."

"Good, but tenga cuidado, Papá. I heard some railroaders say there's oil around the tracks by the bridge. I saw it there too and I don't want you to slip on it or the ice."

"Gracias, hijita. I'm always careful around oil spills. I'll be sure and tell Mr. Maroni where you saw it. Oil spills can cause fires, especially in this dry winter."

*Sleepy better stay awake watching for oil fires*, I thought. We needed Papá to be safe.

Papá pulled the flaps on his cap down over his ears. Then he hugged me and picked up his lantern. "You niños have been doing a good job with the woodpile. I thought we would only have wood for one luminaria this winter, but I think we might be able to have more for our Posadas. No?"

I clapped my hands. "Caroline wants to help us too."

Papá pointed a finger at me and shook it.

"I know. I know," I said. "Like Abuela always says, 'Al amigo y al caballo, no cansarlos.' We won't make Caroline work like a horse. But at least we'll have farolitos, and maybe two luminarias!"

"We'll see."

## CHAPTER 18

# Santa Lucía

## PATRONESS OF LAMPLIGHTERS

**The next few** days everyone was busier than usual at home. Mamá wanted to make a few gifts for our family in New Mexico and for our teacher, so Felícita and I took over cooking tortillas for our family and the store. We also had the newspapers to deliver and payments to collect from our customers. At school, we learned songs for the program, did all our lessons, and took tests. There was little time to prepare for our family Posadas.

On Thursday, I invited Caroline to come to our house after supper to help us make farolitos. I was gathering some brown paper sacks and the candle stubs from the porch just as she came into the yard. "Here, let me take that," I said as she removed her hands from her rabbit-fur muff. Ernesto took her coat and hung it on a nail in the porch.

"What do I do?" she said, rubbing her hands.

"Let's go in the kitchen where it's warmer," I said.

Felícita had just hung the dish towel to dry, and Mamá and Abuela were drinking coffee.

"It's good to see you, Caroline," Mamá said as she pointed for her to have a seat. "Would you like a cup of Ovaltine?"

"No, thank you, Mrs. Sandoval. Maybe later. I'm here to work. My grandpa says it's high time I help Maggie."

My abuela pulled on Mamá's sleeve and whispered, "¿Quién es Maggie?"

"Es Margarita," Mamá whispered back. "Es su nombre en la escuela."

I had forgotten that Abuela didn't know Maggie was my school name.

"I think the first thing we should do is punch designs in the paper bags for the farolitos," I said.

Ernesto fidgeted on the chair until he sat on his knees. "Tell her what they are."

"A farolito is a little light in a paper bag," I said to Caroline.

"Yeah, and we used to put them all around the church-yard in New Mexico," Ernesto chimed in, "and even on our roof when it was Noche Buena."

"Noche Buena is Christmas Eve," I added. "The little lights light the way for the Holy Family."

Caroline glanced around the room as if she were looking for answers. "In the Bible, Joseph, Mary, and Jesus were in Bethlehem. I don't remember them seeing little lights."

"No," Felícita said. "But light is a symbol that guides the Holy Family to people."

"So that's why you put them on your roof," Caroline said. "I never knew about this custom from New Mexico."

I smiled. Caroline had remembered we were from New Mexico, not Mexico. She really was trying to be a better friend. I picked up a paper bag and folded a collar around it. "The first thing is to fold the top down. That will make the bag stronger." I folded the paper sack flat and picked up a sharp pencil. "Then we punch a pattern below the collar. That way when we put a candle inside, the light will shine through." I punched a large star design on the wide side of the bag with the tip of the pencil, and pushed it all the way through the sack. "See what I mean?"

Caroline nodded. "It looks like stitches made by a giant Singer sewing machine."

Everyone laughed as I passed out bags and pencils.

"Save a bag for Alberto," said Ernesto. "He went to the pump house when we left the store. He'll be here pretty soon."

No sooner had Ernesto made the announcement than Alberto came in the kitchen with his guitar. "Here, help us make farolitos," I said to him.

"No, you go ahead. I'll provide the Christmas music until I turn in for the night," he said as he tuned his guitar. He began to play one of my favorite Christmas songs, "Noche de Paz," or as it was called at school, "Silent Night."

About an hour later we had punched designs on all the bags, finished drinking Ovaltine, and sung "Silent Night" to Alberto's accompaniment. First we all sang it in English, and then we sang in Spanish as Caroline listened.

"Now all we have to do is put some dirt in the bags and nestle the candles in it," I said. "The dirt holds down the bags in the wind."

"And we have to light the candles too," Ernesto said. "Just you wait and see how pretty they'll look. Little fires all in a row."

"It's been fun seeing you make the farolitos, but I've got an early shift. So, good night, everybody," Alberto said. He put his guitar pick in the neck of the guitar and went to bed.

"You should ask your brother if he can play for our Christmas program," Caroline said as Ernesto fetched her things from the porch. She put on her coat. "I'll bet Miss Shugart would like that. It would be more special than a pitch pipe."

Ernesto's eyes lit up and he nodded. "It would!"

I shrugged. "I don't know. He just plays for family. He might not want to."

"Well, he shouldn't keep his light hidden," Caroline said.

"Yeah, like our farolitos," Ernesto said as he opened the door for Caroline.

She waved goodbye and started walking down the porch steps. "I'll see you tomorrow." She stopped and ran back. "Oh, I forgot. There's a surprise! Grandpa gave the railroaders and their wives early Christmas gifts. They're at the pump house. That's why he wanted those measurements."

"What are they?"

She smiled. "If I told you, it wouldn't be a surprise."

"They must be big if your grandpa put them in the pump house," I said.

Caroline nodded. "You *have* to come with me to the pump house right after school tomorrow. I want to put a sign up so the railroaders will know how to use the gifts."

"Can my papá and Alberto use them too?"

She rolled her eyes. "Of course they can. They work on the railroad, don't they?"

"Okay, I'll ask if I can go."

The next day, Caroline tugged on her grandfather's arm almost as soon as we arrived at the store after school. "Can I take Maggie to the pump house now? I want to make the signs for . . ." Her voice got softer. "You know what."

He winked and put both hands on her shoulders. "We've got lots of customers, so I need you here for a bit. How about cleaning up in the meeting room?"

"Oh, Grandpa. It stinks in there." She shuddered. "All those cigarette butts and spittoons."

"All right. Man the cash register until the customers thin out."

"Mr. Sims, I can help clean the meeting room," I said.

"That's kind of you, but like Caroline says, it does smell in there."

"I'll wash my hands really good to get the smell off when I'm done."

"Okay. You would be a big help, but no need to touch the spittoons. I'll take care of those."

Caroline handed me the dustpan from behind the door, and I went into the meeting room. Some men sat at tables, talking in the hazy, smoke-filled space. It was just like a song Caroline played sometimes on the Victrola: "Smoke Gets in Your Eyes." I quietly hummed the tune as I pushed chairs back to their places. A hand tapped my shoulder, and I jumped and turned around. It was Alberto.

"You scared me. What are you doing? I thought you were working," I said.

"I worked two shifts yesterday and was pretty tired. Mr. Maroni thought I should take some time off."

"Then why are you carrying your guitar?"

"One of my friends heard I play guitar. He wondered if I could show him a few chords."

"That's good. I'm here sweeping while Caroline works the cash register, and then we're going to the pump house. She says there's a present there for all the railroaders."

"I guess that includes Papá and me?"

I nodded and Alberto started to push in chairs too.

"That's okay. I can do it," I said. "There are quite a few customers for Caroline to help, so I don't need to rush. Could you play 'Silent Night' for me?"

Alberto sat down and strummed some chords. "English or Spanish?"

"English," I said, as I emptied some cigarette butts into the dustpan. Soon, Alberto's soft voice took me away from the haze and stale smell.

Just as I was halfway through sweeping the floor, Mr. Sims and Caroline came into the meeting room with Miss Shugart. Alberto started to stand up.

"No, keep playing," Mr. Sims said, motioning for Alberto to sit down.

Miss Shugart also sat down and put her purse on the table. She listened intently as Alberto played. When he finished "Silent Night," she stood up and clapped. "Absolutely beautiful. Your sisters and brother never mentioned you play the guitar. And your voice is . . . heavenly."

Alberto scratched his neck with his guitar pick. "The

voice might be better if I dropped this habit." He pointed to his cigarette butt in the ashtray. "But I do play a little."

"I'd say you play more than a little," Miss Shugart said as she picked up her purse. "I wish I could play something to accompany the children as they sing for the Christmas program."

"I'm looking forward to hearing them," Alberto said.

"Oh. You're going to be there?"

Alberto knocked his fist lightly on his guitar for luck. "Yes. We usually have evenings off."

Miss Shugart leaned forward. "Would you consider accompanying the children on 'Silent Night'?"

Alberto nodded. "I'd like that."

"I wouldn't expect you to practice with us. I know how busy railroaders are." Miss Shugart clutched her purse. "Good. It's settled. I'll prepare the children, and I know they'll be delighted. Isn't that right, girls?"

Caroline looked at Miss Shugart and nodded. "I told you he was good. The guitar music will make the program so special."

Miss Shugart offered her hand to Alberto and they shook. "Come a little early to the program so you can sit up front. Now if you'll excuse me, I have a bit of shopping to do."

Our teacher left the meeting room, and I emptied the dustpan outside in the oil barrel that served as a trash can.

Inside, Caroline and I finished sweeping the meeting room clean in a few minutes. Then she went in the backroom and came out with her box of crayons and two large pieces of cardboard, cut from a box. Those must be for her signs. We ran to the pump house in the cold, huffing and puffing when we reached it.

"All right, Maggie, stay right here. I'm going in to make the signs. It'll just take a minute. I'll tell you when I'm finished so you can come in and see the surprise. Pinky swear you won't peek?"

"I promise. I won't peek."

The cold wind bit my feet and hands, so I stomped and blew warm breath on my mittens while I waited. What was the surprise—especially one that Papá and Alberto could use?

Finally, Caroline opened the door. "Close your eyes, Maggie. No peeking." She guided me into the front room of the pump house. "You can open your eyes now," she said, clapping her hands.

Right in front of me were two of those new electric washing machines that we unboxed the other day. But that wasn't what made me gasp out loud. The sign on top of one read, in Caroline's penmanship, FOR WHITES ONLY. The other one said, FOR GREASERS ONLY.

## CHAPTER 19

# *Nuestra Señora de los Dolores*
## OUR LADY OF SORROWS

*I felt like* a train hit me in the gut. Tears rushed to my eyes. I squeezed them shut, as if I could wash the hateful words off the signs with my tears.

"Maggie, Maggie, what's wrong? You don't look good."

I forced myself to open my eyes. The signs were still there, and so was Caroline, fanning her hand in front of my face.

For a moment I couldn't speak. Then words spewed out of my mouth in a rush, like the train engines letting off steam. "How could you? How COULD you? I thought you were my friend!"

I ran from the room and out the pump house door. The stinging wind that slapped my face wasn't as cruel as Caroline's signs.

Caroline ran after me. "Maggie, I *am* your friend. What's wrong? Please tell me."

"Leave me alone!" What was wrong? Everything was wrong. Caroline didn't act like a friend. Why did I ever think she was?

When I got home, I went straight to my bedroom. Abuela wasn't there. I flopped backward on the bed, punched the mattress with my fists, and kicked the headboard. How dare Caroline call Papá and Alberto greasers! She was no better than those railroaders in her grandpa's store.

Mamá came into the room, probably because she heard the thumping on the wall. "What's wrong, hijita?"

I turned my face to the wall. She felt my forehead with the back of her hand. I couldn't tell her about the signs. Mamá hardly ever went anywhere in town. Papá, Alberto, Felícita, Ernesto, or I took care of everything. She stayed home with Abuela. She didn't know how people really saw us and what they called us. And if I told her what happened, she'd tell me to forgive and forget.

"I know something is bothering you," Mamá said. "I'll be in the kitchen if you want to talk."

I rolled over on my side. At first, it seemed like the winds blew us to Wyoming. In the summer, the soft breezes cooled us down and perfumed the air with the sweet smell of sagebrush. But as summer turned to fall, the wind got strong again and started pushing. Now the wind seemed even stronger. It kept people from listening to each other. People seemed to only hear what they wanted to hear so they could say what they wanted to say. And what they said hurt us. It reminded me of the dicho, "Quien la fama ha perdido, está muerto aunque vivo." I didn't want anyone to take away our good name.

Mamá was chopping onions when I walked in the kitchen. If I cried some more, I could blame it on them.

"Are you feeling better?" she asked.

"A little bit." I sighed and sat down next to Abuela, who was folding dish towels. "I went to the pump house after school with Caroline. Mr. Sims gave the railroaders two brand-new washing machines."

"How nice." Mamá smiled, put some kindling in the fire box, and lit a match to it.

"Caroline made two signs for the machines. One said that one of the machines is for whites only. The other machine is for greasers only. That's what the signs said."

I waited for a reaction. The only one I got was Mamá going over to the stove with the skillet.

I repeated myself. "Mamá, one machine is *for greasers only.*"

"Oh, that's good. If you can watch your abuela sometimes, maybe I can wash your papá's and Alberto's overalls in it."

I stood up. "No! Don't wash Papá's overalls there." My tears flowed like my words. "Those railroaders don't want Papá and Alberto working here. They want us to go back to New Mexico. I want to go back too."

Mamá came over and hugged and rocked me. "The railroad needs your papá."

"I heard some railroaders at the store. They think Papá and Alberto took jobs away from them. They even called us greasers." I pulled back and looked up at her.

"Those men don't know us," Mamá reminded me. "They call your papá and Alberto names because they don't want to give them credit for their hard work. They're afraid for their own jobs."

"Sí," Abuela said. "Unos cardan la lana y otros agarran la fama."

"But even Caroline thinks we're greasers. She wrote it on the sign," I sobbed.

"Is your name Greaser?" Mamá asked.

"No . . . but . . ."

"Of course it's not. You were named for Santa Margarita because you were born in July near her saint's day, and we wanted you to be strong like her. People persecuted her for being a Christian, but she never turned away from who she was. You know who you are, and it isn't a greaser." Mamá stroked my hair. "Oh, hijita, the word *greasers* can be very ugly, but it can also mean greasy overalls, just the way *whites* can mean white clothes only. I'm sure that's what Caroline meant on the signs. She wouldn't hurt you on purpose. She's your friend."

I wiped my tears. "Do you think so?" I said.

Mamá nodded. "Now set the table so I can finish making supper."

I gathered the forks and spoons from the cupboard. Was Caroline my friend? I wanted to believe that Mamá spoke the truth. Caroline asked me what I wanted to do now, instead of telling me what to do. She came to our house to help us make farolitos and didn't make fun of anything. And even when I thought she said things that could hurt our family or the Martínez family, it ended up that those things were all in my head. I could really trust her. She had become the kind of friend I had wanted since before we came to Wyoming. But that meant I needed to explain to her why I ran away and how the word *greaser* was like a knife to my heart. We needed to figure out how friends talk to each other.

I knew the story of my name but hadn't thought about it for a long time. My parents named me Margarita for a saint they admired. My middle name, Lucia, came from another saint. It meant light. All my family for generations had good, holy names they lived up to, and no one could take that away from us. No one. I had to be strong like Santa Margarita and live up to my name.

CHAPTER 20

# Santa Rita

## INVOKED FOR DESPERATE CAUSES AND ABUSED WOMEN

**Early the next** morning, I took the eggs to the store before the Seventh-day Adventists' Saturday church service. I saw Mr. Sims and Caroline setting up chairs in rows in the meeting room. They didn't see me, so I cleared my throat. "Hello, Mr. Sims," I said, before turning to Caroline. "Caroline, there's something I need to talk to you about."

"You girls go ahead," Caroline's grandfather said. "I'll put away these eggs and check that everything's ready for the church service." He went back into the store, leaving us alone.

Caroline's eyes followed her grandfather as her hands opened and closed. Her voice cracked. "Hi, Maggie."

I cleared my throat. This was hard, but if we were going to be friends, I needed to tell her how I felt. "Caroline, the reason I ran away from you at the pump house yesterday was because my feelings were hurt. You may not know this, but *greasers* is a bad name for us—Hispanic people. When I saw the washing machine with the 'For Greasers Only' sign on top, it felt like a knife went through my heart. I thought you meant it was the only machine my family could use, and the 'Whites Only' machine was for everyone else in town. It was like you were telling us we didn't belong."

Her fingers touched her lips. "I'm really sorry, Maggie. I wouldn't call you a bad name. I just meant that one machine was for greasy overalls, and the other one was for clothes that need to be bleached."

"That's what my mother said it meant, but I wanted to hear it from you. I was so upset. I thought you were my best friend, and I wondered why you would want to hurt me so badly." I realized I was crying.

She whispered, "Thank you for telling me how you feel. We're still friends, aren't we?"

I smiled. "Yes, we're still friends. But friends think before they say things and listen to each other. Maybe we can both do a better job with that. Oh, and another thing: I'd like you to call me my real name from now on. Not Maggie. Margarita."

"I promise," Caroline said, and hugged me like a warm blanket. "But you'll have to remind me when I forget, okay?"

"I will. I better go before your church service starts," I said.

"I'll go over to the pump house today and rewrite those signs," she promised. Then she took my hands in hers and smiled. "I think you know this, but you're the best friend I've ever had. No one else has had as much patience with me as you."

It was my turn to smile.

As I was about to leave, I noticed a man with his head down on the table on the other side of the room. A cigarette smoldered in an ashtray next to him. "Who's that?" I whispered.

"That's Sleepy. When he lifts his head, you'll recognize him." She tried to stop a giggle. "He's a good advertisement for the railroad, because he smokes like a train."

Even though I disliked Sleepy, I put my hand over my mouth to stop my laugh. We moved around the partition and went into the store.

"He's always bragging about how he smokes the same cigarettes the Giants smoke," Caroline said. I must have given her a blank stare, because she explained, "The Giants are the New York Giants, and they won the World Series in baseball. They smoke Camels, according to the ads. All cigarettes stink if you ask Grandma and me, but we sure sell him a lot of Camel cigarettes and Schlitz beer."

I nodded. In the back room, the man began snoring.

When Caroline's grandfather went back into the room, we watched from behind the partition. He went up to Sleepy and shook his shoulders. "Mr. Larsen, we have church services in an hour." The man lifted his head slowly, and Mr. Sims pointed to the smoldering cigarette. "Be sure to dump your cigarette and the ashes in the trash can outside. The missus likes the room to smell fresh, and we don't have flowers for the service."

Sleepy looked like an angry bear being awakened from hibernation. He stood up, bowed to Mr. Sims, and growled, "Whatever you say, Your Highness." He picked up the ashtray and staggered toward the back door.

"Oh, and when you get home, you might make yourself a pot of strong coffee and drink it," Mr. Sims said. "No one wants any accidents on the job."

Sleepy took a long drag on his cigarette as he stomped out of the store.

I went home soon after that, and Felícita and I spent the rest of the morning helping Mamá make tamales. Ernesto was off playing with his friend Sam. By noon I was tired, but we had forty tamales to show for our work. The little pig from our matanza served us well. I had just taken out the poem Ernesto and I were going to say for the program when my little brother skidded into the kitchen.

"There's a fire at the store," he shouted.

Mamá pulled the sheer curtain away from the window, but I couldn't see any smoke rising over the embankment on the other side of the tracks. Mamá put her hands on Ernesto's shoulders. "What happened?" she asked.

Ernesto covered his ears. "The store's on fire. Some men are putting it out. Papá and Alberto are helping and everyone's shouting."

I crossed myself. *Please, God, help Caroline and Mr. Sims be safe.*

## CHAPTER 21

# *La Crucifixión*
## THE CRUCIFIXION

**Mamá wouldn't allow** us to go the store to learn more about the fire. She did say we could lay piles of logs for our luminarias after we ate some tamales. We made one pile by the house and started another one by the road. It was already getting dark when Ernesto shouted, "They're coming! They're coming! The fire must be out."

We ran to meet Papá and Alberto as they crossed the tracks. Their faces were covered in soot. Alberto dragged behind Papá and barely lifted his shoulders as if he were a turtle hiding in its shell.

"Are you all right?" I asked when I saw my brother's hand wrapped up in his railroad bandana.

"His hand got burned," Papá answered.

"How about the Simses?" I asked.

"They're fine. Now go pump some water in a basin for your brother."

Ernesto and I ran to the house and had the water ready when they came into the kitchen. Alberto winced when Mamá unwrapped the bandana.

"Good. There are no blisters," Mamá said.

"Felícita, el vinagre," Abuela said, and my sister hurried to the cupboard to get some vinegar. Mamá poured some hot water from the kettle into a basin of freezing cold water and added apple cider vinegar. She swished the liquids around before gently placing Alberto's hand in the water. He winced again and closed his eyes as he lifted his hand from the basin.

"Keep your hand in the water," Mamá said. "It will help the pain."

Alberto blew out some air, which seemed to relax him, and he put his hand back in the water.

Mamá pushed a lock of hair away from his forehead. "Hijito, tell your boss you need to miss work for a day. We want to keep your hand clean so you don't get any infections."

"That won't be a problem." Alberto locked eyes with Papá. "I was fired."

Mamá's hands flew to her face. My eyes blinked back tears. I could barely hear her ask, "¿Qué pasó?"

Papá threw his cap down on the table. "Tell them what happened, hijo."

Alberto ran the hand that wasn't burned through his hair. "I was supposed to meet Papá at the store, and I came around the back. That's when I saw Sueño. He looked drunk, but he'd set this little pile of newspapers against the back wall of the store, and he dropped a lit cigarette on top of it. I ran over, picked up some dirt, and threw it on the fire to stop it from spreading. It spread anyhow and my coat cuff caught on fire. I slapped at it and finally got my coat off, and then I ran into the store and told Mr. Sims everything." Alberto took a deep breath. "He and about five men in the church came out to help, but when we got there, the fire was even bigger and Sueño punched me in the face. I don't know what got into me, maybe reflexes, but I punched him back. The next thing I knew, people were shouting for us to stop fighting."

"I was waiting for Alberto in front of the store when I heard all the commotion," Papá said. "I went around the back to help fight the fire."

"Sam and I walked by about then," Ernesto said. "That's when I ran home."

Alberto rubbed his forehead. "While the other men put the fire out, Mr. Maroni pulled Sueño away from me and locked his arms behind his back. Another man did the same to me. Sueño kept shouting, 'It's his fault. He started it.' And I shouted back, 'You started it.' We kept going like this until Sueño said, 'This alien started the fire.' Yes, he called me an alien, and some other bad names too. I had to defend our name, so I tried to explain how I saw Sueño start the fire. Mr. Sims took my side because he said Sueño had been smoking and was drunk in the store earlier. He kicked Sueño out then, so he thought the man was trying to get even with him by starting a fire."

Papá exhaled. "It was really ugly. Sueño accused Alberto and me of not being American citizens and taking jobs away from local men. I saw two of the men nodding. Mr. Maroni had to have seen this too. He had no choice but to suspend Alberto, Sueño, *and* me from our jobs because of the fight, and until the railroad investigates the fire and learns if we're Americans."

Felícita's fist almost covered her mouth. "No, Papá! They can't—they can't let you go."

Mamá started shaking and wrung her hands. Papá cradled her in his arms. He stroked her hair, but she cried and cried.

With tears in his eyes, Ernesto said, "I don't want to move. This is our home now."

The word *home* struck me. The store was basically home to Caroline and the Simses. "Is the store all right?" I asked. "The Simses?"

Alberto nodded.

Abuela fingered her rosary that always hung on the side of her dress and began praying the Hail Mary. "Dios te salve, María, llena eres de gracia. El Señor es contigo. . . ."

I joined her in saying the familiar words, and it was as if time stopped. Everyone and everything was silent as we all knelt and prayed the rest of the rosary.

After what seemed like hours, Papá looked up. "God will provide," he said.

I wiped my eyes. *Yes. And God helps those who help themselves.* "Papá is right. God won't forsake us," I said. "We have to have faith." I helped my little brother up. "Do you remember what we were doing when Papá and Alberto came home this evening?"

Ernesto wiped his own tears on his sleeve. "We were piling the wood for the luminarias."

"That's right. We still have more to do to get ready for our Posadas. It's almost the holy season. We should concentrate on getting ready for Christ—together."

"Yes. We need to look for God, not trouble," Papá said. He patted Alberto's shoulder. "Do you think you will be able to strum the guitar for Las Posadas?"

Alberto took his hand out of the basin and nodded. "It's starting to feel better. By Monday I should be good."

"We can put a basin of water near your bed in case you need to cool it overnight," Mamá said.

Ernesto tugged on Mamá's sleeve. "Remember when you had to sleep with your hands in cool water when you peeled the hot chile?"

Mamá raked Ernesto's hair with her fingers. "I didn't sleep that night at all." She handed Alberto a towel to dry his hand.

Mamá brought in a couple of tamales from the cold porch and heated them up for Papá and Alberto. After they nibbled on them, I helped Abuela up from her chair and put her arm in mine as we headed to our bedroom. "Remember, we all have work to do on our Posadas in the morning," I said, giving Ernesto a little swat as he ran past me. Abuela patted my hand and hummed the melody to the song we always sang for Las Posadas.

After I helped Abuela get into bed, I knelt, crossed myself, and prayed.

*Lord, I know you listen to your saints and angels. I invoke them, in your name, to help our family. We are in need of your divine mercy. Amen.*

## CHAPTER 22

# Nuestra Señora de la Luz
## OUR LADY OF LIGHT,
## INVOKED FOR GUIDANCE INTO BATTLE

**Sunday morning I** woke up early. I lay in bed praying that the investigation would prove Alberto didn't start the fire and that Papá and my brother would be able to keep their jobs. Abuela stirred, and we got ready for our trek to the outhouse.

Felícita and Ernesto were in the kitchen when I sat Abuela down to eat breakfast. My sister was fixing oatmeal. She sighed. "I'm going to miss our church in New Mexico and the singing for our Posadas. It won't be the same with just us."

"I can't remember how the song goes," Ernesto said.

"Abuela knows it," I said. I stirred the oatmeal on the stove. "Abuela, would you sing the song for Las Posadas for us?"

She smiled. "Las Posadas es buena para nuestra familia. Traígame agua, por favor."

"Sí, Abuela," I said as I poured her a glass of water.

Abuela sipped some water and then sang the first

verse, where Joseph asks for lodging for Mary and himself in Bethlehem because Mary can't walk any farther. People outside the house would sing it to the people inside.

> "*En nombre del cielo os pido posada*
> *Pues no puede andar mi esposa amada.*"

What beautiful words and music. The tune spun in my memory like the records Caroline played on her phonograph. It made me remember how easy and peaceful everything seemed to be before we moved. Our family was like Joseph and Mary asking the people in Fort Steele to let us in.

"Can you sing more of the song for us so I can write the words down?" I asked.

Abuela nodded. I went into our bedroom and felt around our dresser until I found a pencil and paper. Once I got settled at the kitchen table, she sang two more verses, which I wrote down. In the next one, the innkeeper told Joseph not to bother him, because if Joseph and Mary angered him, he would beat Joseph. People inside the house would sing this verse.

> "*Ya se pueden ir y no molestar*
> *Porque si me enfado voy a apalear.*"

This is exactly what the railroaders at the store wanted to do to us. They wanted to beat us—but with hateful, lying words.

Abuela sang the various innkeepers' words and then Joseph's responses. Near the end of the song, the innkeeper invited Joseph and Mary in, apologizing that he hadn't recognized them.

> "*¿Eres tú, José? ¿Tu esposa es María?*
> *Entren peregrinos, no los conocía.*"

I wanted the message of Las Posadas to come true so our family would be accepted like the innkeeper accepted the Holy Family. A good first step was that Caroline had started to accept my family and me for who we were.

After supper that night, we stayed home. Papá wrote a letter to Abuelita Cruzita, Mamá and Felícita checked on the food for our Posadas, and I asked Abuela to sing the song again, but more slowly, so I could double-check all the words. I copied the song out three times and stacked the papers on the dresser. Now we would all be able to sing the song at our Posadas tomorrow.

## CHAPTER 23

# San Acacio

## INVOKED AGAINST HEADACHES

**Our rooster woke** me early Monday morning. Abuela always used to tell me "Un buen gallo en cualquier gallinero canta" because I didn't like to get up early. Today we really needed to act brave like the good rooster.

With Abuela and Felícita still asleep, I tiptoed out of the room. Mamá stood in the kitchen flipping a tortilla on the comal.

I hugged her. "Buenos días le de Dios, Mamá."

She made the sign of the cross on my forehead and smiled. "Buenos días te de Dios, hijita. You're up early, when you could still be sleeping a little longer."

"Today's our Posadas, so I wanted to make sure we're ready for tonight."

Before we went to school, Papá helped us build our last luminaria. It felt different having Papá and Alberto home on a weekday. We stacked the wood close to the chicken coops in a small pile. There were fewer trees here, so the luminarias were a lot smaller than the bonfires we used to have in New Mexico.

Caroline was already at school when we arrived. She ran to greet us and grabbed my hand. "I'm so excited about going to your house tonight. I've never celebrated a holiday in December other than Christmas."

"This is kind of related to Christmas," I said. "Just wait until you see our luminarias. The fires will help you find our house in the dark."

Caroline smiled, then her face grew concerned. "How's your brother? I saw your dad wrapping up his hand. Did he get burned?"

"Yes, but not too bad, and there weren't any blisters."

"That's good. Grandpa was glad people helped put out the fire, but he was worried they'd get hurt too."

"I'm glad you and your grandparents are okay and that the fire was small," I said. "Did you hear everything that happened?"

"Just parts."

I started to cry. Caroline put her arm around my shoulder and handed me her handkerchief. "Don't cry. Alberto's going to be fine."

I blew my nose. "His hand will get better, but will he get his job back? Will we be able to hold our heads up?" Caroline looked puzzled. I explained, "That man, Sleepy, accused my brother of starting the fire. Alberto got in a fight with him. Then Sleepy said my dad and brother weren't US citizens. Now both of them are suspended from their jobs."

"That's terrible. What happens next?" Caroline asked.

"The railroad is investigating the fire and whether Papá and Alberto are citizens and can keep working. If they don't get to keep their jobs, we'll have to move back to our old home in New Mexico. I know Papá. He'll make us move before the railroad gets a chance to fire him."

Tears welled up in Caroline's eyes and she squeezed my hand. "Oh, Maggie . . . Margarita. You can't go back. You're the best friend I've ever had." She smiled through her tears. "You know I'll help you any way I can."

Abuela often said, "Más vale un amigo que mil parientes, ellos lejos y él presente." It meant a friend nearby could be worth more than a thousand relatives who lived far away. Caroline was truly my friend.

Miss Shugart rang the bell, and everyone lined up along the outside wall of the school. She came to where my sister and brother and I were standing. "How's your brother? I heard he got hurt."

"He got some burns on his hand," Felícita said, "but he's better now."

"Yeah. It's a good thing the burns are on the back of one hand and not on his fingers," Ernesto said. "He said he'll still play for our program."

Miss Shugart put her hand on her chest. "That's a real blessing."

After we finished our regular schoolwork, we practiced for the Christmas program. Miss Shugart announced that Alberto would be accompanying us on "Silent Night." The other kids buzzed, and I could hear comments like, "Wow!" and "Wish I could play the guitar." Hearing these words made me sit up a little taller, and I saw that Felícita and Ernesto did the same thing.

At the end of the day, Miss Shugart reminded us there was no school the next morning. She gave herself Tuesday morning off because she said she'd be working Wednesday evening at our program.

As we were leaving school, I told Caroline, "Don't eat supper at home. My mother's been cooking for weeks and our icebox is full."

"Sounds good! I'll see you later," Caroline said as she skipped to the store.

★ ★ ★

That evening we lit our four piles of luminarias. Felícita and I carried a bucketful of dirt to the porch to fill the paper bags for our farolitos. We had scooped dirt into almost all the bags when Caroline knocked at the door.

"I had no trouble seeing your house when I crossed the

tracks—even without the moon," she said. "Your bonfires are so bright! What do you want me to do?"

I dusted the dirt off my hands. "You can help us put the votive candles in the bags."

We carried the bags outside and spaced them out to make a path to the house, starting from the chicken coop.

"What do you call these again?" Caroline asked.

"They're farolitos."

"That's really a pretty name," Caroline said.

"They're even prettier when they're lit."

For once the wind wasn't blowing, and we were able to light the candles with matches, even though we had to stop and blow on our hands now and then in the cold. When we were done, we watched the glow of the luminarias and farolitos in the yard for a while. They reminded me of the votive candles in the niche of the old church in El Carmen where we asked God to answer our prayers. I could feel Him here too, and I said a quick prayer. Then we went inside, and I helped warm the tortillas on the comal and stirred the pot of posole on the stove. The aroma of beans, tamales, and hominy stew in red chile circled the room like warm hugs.

"Ay, hijitos," Papá said, pulling up his suspenders. "It's like being home again."

"It is home," Ernesto said, dancing around the room.

*I'm not so sure about that*, I thought, but I reminded

myself to have faith. I picked up the copies of the Las Posadas verses I had written down and passed them out. "I think Papá, Alberto, Ernesto, and I should be the Holy Family. We have the warmest coats. Abuela, Mamá, and Felícita can be the innkeepers." I looked at Caroline. "You can stay inside with the innkeepers or go outside with us, the Holy Family."

"I'll go with you," she said.

Papá, Alberto, Ernesto, Caroline, and I put our coats on, and Papá grabbed two flashlights. We walked out the door to the farthest luminaria by the chicken coop and began humming the tune to Las Posadas. As we walked from the yard to the house, we could see Mamá, Felícita, and Abuela inside. By the time we got to the door, the melody had become familiar enough that Caroline could hum along with our singing.

Papá gave me a flashlight. He knocked, and the innkeepers opened the door. After we sang the first verse, Caroline whispered. "What does that mean?"

I whispered back. "'In the name of heaven I ask you for lodging.' *Posada* means lodging. The second line is, 'Well, my beloved wife cannot walk.'"

Abuela's voice sounded strong and clear as she led the innkeepers in their part, where they told the Holy Family there wasn't room for them in the inn. We continued singing back and forth, plea and rejection, as we stood by the door. Even though it was cold, it was fun to see

Caroline trying to sing the words of the song in Spanish.

Finally, when the innkeepers invited us inside, everyone sang:

> "*Entren santos peregrinos, peregrinos reciban este*
> *    rincón,*
> *Que aunque pobre la morada, la morada, os la doy de*
> *    corazón.*"

As soon as we finished singing and the last notes died away, Ernesto called out, "Let's eat!"

We all laughed. The kitchen felt warm and inviting. It gave me the same feelings I had when we first moved to Fort Steele and believed we would be welcomed by people in this town.

Alberto went to put out the fires while the rest of us readied for dinner. I made sure to point out to Caroline that the posole had pork.

"I can just eat the hominy," Caroline said.

I shook my head. "But it's cooked in pork broth."

"You're stricter about my religion than we are." She sighed. "Okay, I'll just have some beans and tortillas."

I served Caroline a bowl of beans. The rest of my family probably looked like a small church gathering eating giant hosts for communion as we dunked our tortillas in the posole.

For dessert, Caroline helped herself to a pumpkin empanada. "This is kind of like a pumpkin pie turnover. That's Grandma's favorite pie." She looked up, closed her eyes, and tapped her chin. "Hmmm. I wonder if these would sell. . . ."

I shook my head and wagged my finger at Caroline. "We're already busy with tortillas, newspapers, and eggs."

We all laughed. Later Caroline ate three biscochitos while I nibbled on one.

"I guess I better go. It's getting really late," Caroline said, and grabbed another biscochito. Mamá wrapped four pumpkin empanadas in waxed paper for her to take home.

"Mamá, I'm going to walk Caroline to the tracks," I said.

"Por favor, check on the luminarias and farolitos," Papá said. "I want to make sure they're out."

"I'll check too," Alberto said and went to the porch to get his coat.

As Caroline and I walked down the steps, snow began to fall. It dusted the ground like the sugar on the biscochitos. "That was really fun and different," Caroline said. "I'm glad I got to come." We stopped where Alberto was checking the logs, then picked up sticks and poked the logs of the closest luminaria too. "I don't see any embers anywhere," Caroline said.

"I don't see any either," Alberto agreed.

Just to be sure, I kicked dirt onto the woodpiles as we walked. "Thanks for coming," I said when we reached the farthest little bonfire.

"Maybe you can come to the store tomorrow and teach me parts of the song," she said, putting her hands in her white muff, "especially since we don't have school in the morning."

"Sure. I'd like that. I'll ask if I can stay a while after I bring the eggs."

It was cold now and the wind picked up, so after waving goodbye, I ran back to the house. Alberto was still checking on the fires.

## CHAPTER 24

# San Florián
## INVOKED AGAINST FIRES

**Before the rooster** crowed, I heard a loud knocking on the front door. I got out of bed, grabbed a wool blanket from the trunk, and wrapped it around my shoulders. When I reached the parlor, I found Papá buttoning his flannel shirt and Alberto combing down his hair with his fingers. When Papá opened the door, I saw it had snowed a few inches last night, and a strange truck sat in the yard outside. I squinted to see the words on the side of the truck that said UNION PACIFIC. What did the railroad want so early in the morning? Was this the investigation into the fight?

Two men were standing on the porch. The taller man asked, "Is this where Alberto Sandoval lives?"

Alberto pointed to himself. "Yes."

"We have a few questions for you," the man continued.

Papá let the men in, but they didn't take off their hats. Mamá and Felícita joined us in the parlor.

"We're investigators for the railroad. Name's Smith.

Nick Smith. This here's Bob Davidson," the tall man said, nodding to the shorter man. "There was a fire last night. The wind spread it so quickly, no one could stop it. It burned down the old army barracks—the one where Leo Maroni lives."

Papá looked dazed. "My boss's house? Is he all right?"

They nodded.

"What time?" Papá asked.

"'Bout three A.M. We got a report that you had bonfires in your yard last night," Mr. Smith said. "We're just trying to see if there's any connection."

Oh my gosh! Was someone blaming the fire on us?

Papá said, "Yes, we had some small bonfires last night for a family celebration. Our eldest son checked to make sure they were out before we went to bed."

"What time was that?" Mr. Smith asked.

Papá looked at Mamá. "About ten o'clock?"

Mamá nodded.

"Excuse me," I said, looking up at Mr. Smith. "My friend and I checked the fires too and saw my brother checking them. They were out."

"Well, we've just started investigating all our leads," Mr. Davidson said. He took a notepad from his shirt pocket and licked the tip of his pencil. "What's your friend's name, in case we need some witnesses?"

"Caroline Sims," I said. "She's Bill Sims's daughter.

Sometimes she stays with her grandparents at the Sims store. She'll tell you the fire was out." I knew Caroline would tell the truth if the investigators asked her.

The man wrote down the information. "Thank you for your help," he said to me. "We may need to talk to you again, and to your friend."

"Who made the report about our fires?" I asked.

Mr. Smith looked at me. "The man who lives in the bridge tender's house—Peter Larsen."

*Sleepy!* I thought. That man wanted to hurt us any way he could.

"You do know that my brother and Mr. Larsen got in a fight on Saturday?" Felícita said. "And Mr. Larsen was also mad at Mr. Maroni," she added.

They both nodded. "We're aware of that, young lady. That's why we're asking questions." Mr. Smith said. He looked at Alberto. "Your father said you checked on the fire. Is that correct?"

"Yes. I was outside when my sister walked her friend to the tracks."

"What did you do after you checked the fires?"

"I went to bed." Alberto pointed toward his and Ernesto's bedroom. "I share the room with my little brother, but he was already asleep when I got into bed." He opened the door for the men and grabbed his coat from the hook in the porch. "I'll show you where I put out the fires."

I watched from the window as Alberto walked the men around and pointed to the places where the luminarias had burned out. They kept talking for a long time. Finally I saw Alberto throw his hands up in the air, and the men got in their truck, revved up the engine, and drove away.

Alberto entered the house and stomped his feet on the rug near the door.

Ernesto came out of their room and rubbed his eyes. "What happened?"

"The barracks burned down—Mr. Maroni's house," Papá said. "Those men were railroad investigators, asking questions about it."

"Yes," Alberto said. "And they want me and Papá to meet with them and some other railroad men later today. They think I started that fire."

Ernesto started to cry. "You wouldn't start a fire."

"No," Papá said as he shut the screen door. "He didn't start it, but I'd like to find out who did."

★ ★ ★

Early that morning, Ernesto and I passed by the barracks on our way to the store with some eggs. Our mouths fell open at what we saw. Only the stone foundation of the barracks remained, and the ashes were still smoldering.

We hurried to the store. You would never have known there was a fire there the previous Saturday. Since there was no school that morning, Caroline was surrounded by kids and their moms buying things. Mr. Sims was helping other kids pick out new handkerchiefs and bright red suspenders, probably for the Christmas program tomorrow. People were so busy talking it sounded like a flock of magpies gossiping.

I reached the counter during a lull. Caroline pulled me aside. She whispered, "Margarita, the fire investigators were here before you came. I told them how the snow had already started putting out the fires before we kicked dirt on them, and your brother was checking too. I talked to them in front of my dad. He said he'd go to their meeting this afternoon. I hope it will help Alberto."

"Thank you. I think it will," I said. "Let me help you clean up the back room." The only way for me to put aside my worrying about Papá and Alberto was to pray and keep busy.

"Thanks," Caroline said, handing me the broom.

In the back room, she emptied almost-full coffee cups into a basin and threw the coffee grounds outside. I swept cigarette butts across the floor while the clock slowly ticked away the time. As I swept, I looked around the hazy, smoke-filled room, and an idea came to me.

"Caroline, let's go to the barracks. We have time before

school starts this afternoon," I said. "I have an idea that might help Alberto."

Caroline's eyes got big. "Sure, just let me finish dusting the shelves."

When Caroline's jobs were done, I grabbed Ernesto's hand, and the three of us ran back to the old barracks.

"There's nothing here," Caroline said. "Everything's burned up."

"Look for a Camel cigarette," I said. "That's what Sleepy smokes. He started the fire at the store with a cigarette, and maybe he started this one the same way."

Caroline looked at me but didn't say anything. There had been about four inches of hard-packed snow on the ground when we went to bed last night, and it had snowed more overnight. Still, the snow around the base of the barracks was muddy and tramped down, probably from the heat and the men trying to put the fire out. We searched around the barracks until Caroline finally threw her hands in the air. "We better go home and eat lunch before school. Maybe the investigators will find something."

"Just a little bit more time, and then we'll go," I promised.

We went around the barracks a second time. I saw something that looked like a short gray stick against the bright white snow. "I found a cigarette!"

Ernesto and Caroline ran over. "Let me see. Let me see!" Ernesto said.

I picked it up and examined it, then held it out to show them. "It's just a Lucky Strike. Well, let's go eat lunch."

As we started walking back to town, Ernesto sniffed the air. "Wait. What's that smell?"

"You're smelling the smoldering ashes," Caroline said.

"No. I've smelled that smell before. It's . . . It's . . . I know! It smells like the gas we put in Claudette."

"What are you talking about?" Caroline said.

"Claudette is the name of Alberto's car," I said.

Caroline and I stopped and breathed in deeply. We nodded. "It does smell like gasoline," she said.

"If Sleepy wanted to start a fire, he might have brought gasoline up from his house and poured it on the barracks," I said. "Let's see if there are fresh footprints coming from his place."

We walked back to the barracks, then around to the side closest to the bridge tender's house. When we looked carefully at the ground, we saw a single set of footprints going to and from Sleepy's house, their edges softened by last night's snow. The footprints weren't very deep, so the investigators might not have seen them in the early morning light.

"Let's follow the path," I said. "Be sure to keep your feet off the trail. Walk on the side."

We followed the footprints about halfway to Sleepy's house. As we passed a sagebrush, I spied an odd square lump underneath it with some black marks showing through the snow. I stooped down to get a closer look. "A whole pack of Camel cigarettes! They're still inside!" Caroline and Ernesto ran over.

"The pack must have fallen out of his pocket," Caroline said. "It's on top of the old snow, but under the new snow."

"That means he must have walked this way last night," I said.

Ernesto pumped his fists in the air. "Alberto didn't start the fire."

"Let's take the pack to the investigators," I said.

Caroline shook her head. "No. Leave it here. You aren't supposed to take evidence away from the scene of the crime. Remember that Sherlock Holmes story we read?"

I stood up slowly. "You're right, but we need to tell someone."

"I'll bet Grandma knows where the investigators are meeting. Daddy and Grandpa are there," Caroline said. "Let's go back to the store."

We ran toward town. From a distance we saw Mr. Maroni. He dragged his feet as he headed into the store.

"Shouldn't he be at the investigators' meeting?" Caroline said.

"You would think so. He's the boss."

"Maybe he's too tired from trying to put out the fire," Ernesto said.

"Yes, maybe that's why," I said. "Let's go tell him what we know."

Mrs. Sims was pouring Mr. Maroni a cup of coffee by the time we got to the back room. He smelled like smoke—fire smoke. It looked like his whiskers grew in overnight. He gave us a tired smile when he saw us in the door. "Margarita, isn't it? And Ernesto and Caroline."

"That's right," I said. "Excuse me, sir. We're glad you're safe, but we're sorry you lost your house."

Caroline and Ernesto nodded.

"Thank you," Mr. Maroni said. "It's only a house. I'll find another one not so close to the tracks next time. I'm just glad my family wasn't home." He rubbed his chin and shook his head. "I don't believe your brother started it."

"Sir, we think someone started the fire on purpose," I said.

He and Mrs. Sims raised their eyebrows.

"And it wasn't my brother," I continued. "The three of us just got back from looking at your house, or what *was* your house."

"It smells funny there too," Ernesto said. "Even though there's smoke, we smell another smell—gasoline."

"We found some footprints and followed them along a path toward the bridge tender's house," I added. "That's where we found a pack of Camel cigarettes. From the snow, it looks like they were dropped overnight."

"We left it there for evidence, just like they do in the Sherlock Holmes books," Caroline said.

Mr. Maroni sat up straight and combed his hair with his hand. "Thanks. Then the investigators should be able to find it." He looked puzzled. "But how do Camel cigarettes prove anything?"

"Leo, there's only one fellow in town who smokes Camels," Mrs. Sims said with her hands on her hips. "We all know that's Sleepy. He's always bragging about how he smokes what the World Series champs smoke. The rest of the fellows smoke Lucky Strikes."

"Alberto smokes . . . What does he smoke?" Ernesto said, looking at me for the answer.

"Our brother is trying to quit smoking, but he rolls his own cigarettes," I said.

"I can vouch for that," Mrs. Sims said. "I sell gum to Mr. Sandoval now, but I used to sell him cans of Prince Albert tobacco. We still sell Sleepy his Camels. Sorry to say this, but my mister also sold Sleepy some Schlitz beer on Friday, and that started the problems we had with *our* fire."

Mr. Maroni rubbed his whiskers. "Sleepy *was* angry with me on Saturday when I sided with Alberto. You say you smelled gasoline?" He looked at me. "Where exactly did you see that pack of cigarettes?"

I told him, and he stood up, drank a swig of coffee, and put the cup down. "Thanks for the coffee, Mrs. Sims, but I better head over to the investigators' meeting. I have some news to share."

## CHAPTER 25

# San Judas Tadeo
## PATRON OF LOST CAUSES

**As Ernesto and** I walked home for lunch, I prayed that our information would be able to clear Alberto's name. I also prayed that wherever Papá and Alberto were meeting with the railroaders, they had some friends besides Caroline's father, grandfather, and Mr. Maroni. We needed all the friends we could get. Maybe Santa Claus would become another friend. He should have received my second letter by now, but just to be sure, I could ask him at the program tomorrow to help us. After all, he was a saint.

Between the excitement of the program and the investigators' meeting going on, I couldn't concentrate in school that afternoon. Once it ended, Ernesto and I ran home across the tracks.

Papá and Alberto weren't home yet, and Mamá and Abuela hadn't heard any news. Ernesto and I practiced "A Visit from Saint Nicholas" again and again, but we both got distracted watching out the window for Papá and Alberto. Mamá and Felícita set the table for dinner.

Finally, we saw them entering the yard, and Ernesto ran to open the door for them. They were both chewing gum, so I couldn't tell from their expressions if they were upset or happy when they came in the kitchen. Mamá scooted everyone to our chairs. The moment the blessing was said, Mamá passed Papá the beans and asked, "¿Qué pasó?"

Ernesto and I leaned forward. "What did they say at the meeting?" I asked.

"They had lots to say after Leo took the investigators on the path near the barracks. Do you know what they found there?"

Ernesto tapped the table as if it were a drum. "A pack of Camel cigarettes."

"How did you know?" Alberto asked.

Ernesto had a grin on his face. "Margarita, Caroline and I did some investigating like . . . What's his name in that book, Margarita?"

"Sherlock Holmes," I said. "First we went to the barracks this morning, because I had a hunch we might find a Camel cigarette there—the kind Sleepy smokes."

Papá pointed his fork at me. "You shouldn't have gone to the barracks without telling someone. It could have been dangerous."

"We just walked around the outside. We were really careful," Ernesto said. "But we didn't find anything right there, did we, Margarita?"

I shook my head, and Ernesto continued describing our investigation. "We followed new footprints in the fresh snow. And then Margarita saw a fresh pack of Camel cigarettes underneath a sagebrush." He wagged his finger. "But we didn't touch it."

"We ran back to the store to tell someone," I said. "Mr. Maroni was just going in, so we told him what we found."

Alberto put his coffee cup down. "Ah, so that's why he came in late to the meeting. The next thing we knew, the two investigators followed Leo out the door. When they came back, the meeting continued. Leo asked Sueño to tell us the kind of cigarettes he smokes. I don't think he wanted to answer, but Leo asked him again. Finally, Sueño said, 'I smoke Camels—so?' Mr. Sims, from the store, stood up and said that the other smokers in town buy Lucky Strikes, except me, and I buy Prince Albert in the can. Then Leo showed everyone the fresh pack of Camels. He said he and the investigators found it on the path from the barracks to the bridge tender's house." Alberto stood up and poured himself another cup of coffee. "And what do you think they found in the back of his house?"

Ernesto looked at me and I looked at him. We both shrugged.

"An empty gasoline can," Alberto said.

"Sueño was angry," Papá said. "He started shouting, 'Someone put it there—probably those kids or hobos trying to keep warm!' But Leo reminded everyone that no one is allowed on that railroad property except the bridge tender. And there was only one set of footprints in the snow leading to the house. Mr. Sims told everyone about all the evidence that Sueño started the fire at the store too. When I looked around the room, the men were nodding. I knew then that they knew Alberto didn't start this fire, but I wasn't sure what the investigators thought."

"The two railroad investigators excused themselves to the back of the room to talk," Alberto said. "When they got up, Sueño did too, but both Mr. Sims and Leo held him down."

"The investigators only talked about three minutes," Papá said. "When they came back they said, 'We clear Alberto of any charges made against him.'" He blew out a long breath.

Mamá reached up and gave Alberto a kiss on the cheek. He walked over and put his arm around me. "I got lots of handshakes and pats on the back, and Mr. Maroni told Papá and me to report to work tomorrow. He told us you were a good detective for a kid. You sure helped me."

"What happened to Sueño?" Ernesto asked.

Alberto shrugged and shook his head ever so slightly. "He was fired and will serve some time in jail for starting the fires. Then he's supposed to stay away from liquor so he can find another job."

Mamá shook her head and sighed. "I'm thankful you both have your jobs back."

Papá lowered his eyes, took a deep breath, and let it go. "We still have another problem."

We all looked at him.

"Alberto and I need to prove we were born in the United States. The railroad investigators would not take our word for it. They said our names prove we're from Mexico. 'Names like yours didn't die for the United States,' is what they said. 'If you're from Mexico, why should you have a job in the United States? Only citizens can keep their jobs.'"

"But you were both born in the United States! Our ancestors too," Felícita insisted.

Alberto stood up and paced the room. "We know that, but how are we going to prove it? We only have our records of baptism from church, and they won't accept those. Even if there are state records, we don't have time to go to Santa Fe and get them."

Ernesto's eyes lit up. "We could use Mr. Sims's telephone and call someone."

Papá shrugged his shoulders. "Who would we call? We'd have to find family in Santa Fe, and we don't know their numbers. Besides, like Alberto said, we probably don't have official records there."

"What did Mr. Maroni say?" Mamá asked as she stood up and took his plate.

Papá spoke softly. "He's on our side, but he heard some people like us got deported to Mexico because they didn't have visas or couldn't prove they were United States citizens. I guess my compadre was right to be worried after all."

Ernesto stood up and put his arms around Papá's neck. "I won't let them take you," he cried.

I put my arms around Papá too. "I won't let them deport you either," I said. Papá rocked us in his arms.

Abuela cleared her throat. "I can help. Recuerdo cuando nacieron tú y Alberto."

"Gracias, Mamá," Papá said as he shook his head. "I know you were there when Alberto was born. I didn't know you saw me too."

"Claro que sí. Su mamá era mi prima."

Papá scratched his head. "Even so, since you're related to me, I don't think they'll take your word for it."

Alberto shook his head. "If we could just show them we had someone who fought in a war for the United States, they'd be convinced. They're always bragging about how *this* relative fought in World War I, and *that* relative came to Fort Steele after the Civil War."

"Well, Abuela Cruzita's father fought in the Civil War," I reminded him. "I even remember his name. It was José del Carmel Cardenas."

"But we can't prove it," Alberto said.

I looked at him and at the others around the table. "Maybe we can't prove that yet, but I know something that might help." I went in the bedroom, pulled Abuelita Cruzita's box from under the bed, and brought it to the table. "These are Abuelita Cruzita's important papers."

We opened up the box. "Look, a death certificate for Abuelo," Alberto said, "with New Mexico listed as his place of birth. That proves your father was born in the United States, Papá."

"Anyone born here is a US citizen, and children of citizens are citizens," Felícita said. "We learned that from Miss Shugart."

Alberto whistled. "And if they say New Mexico is the same as Mexico, we remind them that in 1912, New Mexico became the forty-seventh state."

"I think we have all the proof we need to stay here, thanks to everyone's help," Papá said. He caught my eye and smiled. "We'll show these to Leo Maroni tomorrow."

## CHAPTER 26

# San José

## PATRON OF WORKERS

**On Wednesday morning,** my classmates and I moved our desks to the outside edges of the room. We spent the rest of the day practicing for our Christmas program and decorating the school. Miss Shugart had all of us cut red, green, and white paper into strips. We glued the strips into circles to make long chains that we draped around the room. The Christmas tree that we decorated with strung popcorn and cranberries stood next to the door. After we were done, I stood back and admired how we had trans-formed a regular schoolroom into a festive room.

When school was dismissed, we ran home to see if there was any news. Papá and Alberto hadn't come home yet, but Mamá wanted us to eat an early dinner before the program. When we were almost finished setting the table, Ernesto clinked two spoons together as if it were a signal. Then he and I said all the lines of "A Visit from Saint Nicholas" without the paper in front of us. Mamá and Abuela clapped their hands. Felícita had a half smile on her face, and her eyes said we did a good job. Ernesto and I bowed and then finished setting the table.

The porch screen door slammed, and I ran to see who it was.

"Oh, it's only you," I said, as Alberto wiped his feet on the rug.

He laughed. "Who were you expecting? Your Santa Claus?"

"No, I thought you were Papá."

We walked into the kitchen. Alberto kissed Mamá and Abuela.

"Have you heard anything? Did you talk to Mr. Maroni?" Mamá said as she wrung her hands.

Alberto nodded his head. "Papá is still talking to him. He'll be a little late, but he wants to tell you the news." He looked happy, so I relaxed a bit.

"You kids better eat. We don't want to be late for your program," Mamá said.

"I'm not hungry," I said, looking at the window, hoping Papá would come soon.

"Eat something so you don't get sick," she insisted.

"I'm just a little nervous about everything," I said.

Mamá nodded. "You can eat with Papá when he comes home."

Papá still had not returned by the time we hung the last dish towel to dry. We changed our clothes.

Felícita wore a red dress Mamá had sewn for her. Ernesto wore his wool sweater over his denim shirt and overalls. I slipped on Felícita's dark blue polka-dotted dress, since she had outgrown it. It looked like some of the newer dresses in the Simses' store. Mamá fluffed out the two puffed sleeves and tied the bow in the back where I couldn't reach. The dress swished against my legs as I paced the floor in time to the ticking of the clock. I silently prayed, *Come home, Papá, come home, Papá,* like the rhythm the train made on the tracks.

Then we heard steps on the porch. Ernesto ran to the screen door. "I knew you'd come in time. I just knew it!" he shouted.

I helped Papá take off his denim coat lined with red plaid flannel. It still smelled like smoke. "Come and eat," Mamá said. "Your dinner's still warm." She heated some water in the basin so Papá could wash and then took his plate and one for me out of the oven.

"What did you learn?" Mamá asked.

Papá put his hand up. "I'll tell you, but let me sit down first."

He sat down. We all leaned forward. He smiled. "We've always known our ancestors have been citizens of the United States, and so are we. And now, thanks to Margarita, the railroad people know it too. You should have seen their eyes when I showed them proof that we have an ancestor who fought in the Civil War." He pulled on his suspender straps and paused. "And more good news. Starting next week, I'm going to be the foreman in charge of the men who work on the section. Leo made it official today."

Ernesto jumped up and down, and Felícita and I smothered Papá with hugs and kisses. Papá walked over to Alberto and put his arm around his shoulders. "The foreman is allowed to hire his workers, and so my first duty is to rehire my son."

Mamá dabbed the corners of her eyes with her apron until Alberto gave her his handkerchief.

"I'll earn more money too," Papá said. "Gracias, hijita, for letting me know about the oil spills." He walked over and kissed my forehead. "Leo says you should come work for railroad management—the way you solved the mystery. You helped him make our case. Now I get to be in the driver's seat instead of carrying the load. Isn't that how the dicho goes, Mamá?"

"Sí," Abuela said, and repeated the dicho: "Vale más arrear que no la carga llevar."

"One more mystery. Before they told me I was going to be the foreman, Caroline's dad said someone wrote a letter to the railroad management about Alberto and me the other day. The letter said we were good workers and we had a hard-working family. But I don't know who wrote it," Papá said. He scratched his head. "I'm just thankful someone noticed we can do the job as well as any other men on the railroad. We've proved that our gente are good workers and that we belong here. I even think someday we'll get better jobs on the railroad too."

"Like engineer?" Ernesto said, pulling his arm down like an engineer tooting the whistle.

"Yes, like engineer or conductor. But the most important thing is, we still have our good name," Papá said.

"Whoever wrote the letter must be a saint," Mamá said.

"Maybe it was Santa Claus," Alberto said. He looked at me. "You said you wrote to him and asked him to help the family."

I nodded and Ernesto's eyes got really wide. "It was him. I know it was him," I said.

"Speaking of letters, Ernesto, get the envelope from my jacket," Papá said. "Mr. Sims gave it to me before I came home." When he held it up, we all knew who it was from—Abuelita Cruzita. We could see her flowery hand-writing. Papá took a letter from the envelope, cleared his throat, and read it.

*December 10, 1934*
*Dear family,*

*I am very busy and do not write you for long time. Your tío drive me to Mora this week to pay my taxes. He say I can wait to pay in spring. I say no. I will pay early*

*because la familia help me earn the money. This is our*
*Sandoval land and we will work hard always to keep it*
*for la familia.*

 *Margarita, show your teacher my papers that I*
*send. Tell her you have pride in your bisabuelo who fight*
*in Civil War.*

 *Now the taxes are paid. Now I will come this*
*spring. Blanca will stay here and be ready for you if you*
*visit.*

 *Con mucho amor,*
 *Mamá y Abuelita*


Papá handed me the envelope. I reached inside, pulled out two crackly papers, read them, and smiled. "Here's proof that our ancestor fought for the United States," I said.

 Ernesto and I rushed to hug Papá. He laughed. "Enough, enough. I want to say something. Mamá was able to pay her taxes early thanks to the hard work everyone has done. Alberto and I saved money from our pay. Ernesto and Margarita collected and sold the eggs. Felícita and Josefita, you made delicious tortillas. All of us grew the vegetables, and the three of you delivered papers."

 I looked around the room. Felícita tossed her dark curls back, and Mamá reached for Alberto's handkerchief. Alberto looked like a soldier standing at attention, and Abuela's hands were clasped together as if she were praying.

"I'm proud of our familia." Papá looked at each of us with glistening eyes. "Alberto and I have our jobs back and I'll be making more money, but we want your abuelita to be able to count on each of us to help her pay the taxes each year. This is for the land that will be yours someday, niños, if you ever decide to go back."

"We'll get the money, Papá," Ernesto said, grinning. He rubbed his hands together. "When Abuelita visits, I want her to come on a passenger train."

Papá nodded. "We can't take off work to drive her here, so . . . Yes. She *will* ride the train. Now we need to save money for a train ticket."

Mamá looked at the clock. "You've got to get ready for the Christmas program," she said, shooing everyone out of the kitchen. "Margarita, get the shirt you ironed for your papá. It's hanging in the wardrobe."

"I'll get it," I said. "I just need to do something first."

I went into our bedroom, knelt in front of Abuela's little altar, and bowed my head.

*Thank you, God, for blessing our familia. Abuelita can keep her land now. And I give thanks for Santa Claus. I know he wrote the letter that helped Papá and Alberto keep their jobs. He is my other patron saint now. Amen.*

Then I hurried and gave Papá his shirt. I could hardly wait to say thank you to Santa Claus in person.

## CHAPTER 27

# San Nicolás
## PATRON OF CHILDREN

**Papá changed his** shirt and put on a different coat. Abuela wanted to come to school to hear us, but since the car still wasn't fixed, she decided to stay home, because it was too hard to walk that far. So everyone but Abuela followed the path through the wispy snow to the schoolhouse.

On the walk, Papá said, "After the meeting today, Mr. Smith said, 'Can your wife teach my wife how to make tortillas?'" He laughed. "I told him 'Sure,' and then Caroline's dad said, 'My Caroline can teach her too.' He and I had a good laugh, but we all know it's true."

Alberto nodded. "A couple of men said they were glad their wives were making their lunches with the tortillas they bought at the store. They said it was easier to hold a wrapped tortilla than a sandwich, especially when they're trying to run a big locomotive."

"Leo said he fought in France during World War I," Papá said. "He learned to like goat cheese there. He said he's thinking about getting a goat—but he may need some help with the milking and learning to make the cheese." Papá poked me in the ribs. "What do you niños think?"

"Sure. We could do that," I said, and Felícita and Ernesto nodded.

When we got to the school, Miss Shugart shook hands with Papá, Mamá, and Alberto at the door. "It's so good to see you here tonight, Mr. and Mrs. Sandoval. Your children are such good students."

"Thank you," Papá said. "They work very hard."

Our teacher nodded and pointed to the rows of benches set up in the middle of the room. She whispered to Alberto, "Please have a seat up front. The children are so excited to sing with guitar accompaniment. The program will start very soon."

"I see tu amiga," Mamá said to me, pointing to Caroline and her father. "Give me your coat."

I cleared my throat when I got near them. "Hello, Mr. Sims," I said. "Hi, Caroline."

"You girls go ahead and get ready," Caroline's father said. "I'll check that all the benches are lined up the way Miss Shugart wants them."

I whispered in Caroline's ear, "Is Santa Claus here yet? I want to talk to him."

"He's not here yet. He always comes at the end of the program. Don't worry, you won't miss him."

We took our places at the front of the school. I stood in the back row next to Felícita. I felt almost as tall as my sister. It's funny how tall you can feel when you're happy.

The program began with all eight grades singing "Santa Claus Is Coming to Town." Then Ernesto and I recited "A Visit from Saint Nicholas." Felícita, Joe, and Helen from the eighth grade read the story of the nativity from the Gospel of Luke. The first through third grades sang "Away in a Manger," and the fourth through seventh grades sang "O Come, All Ye Faithful"—even the last verse in Latin.

Before the last song of the program, Miss Shugart announced, "Ladies and gentlemen, we have a very special treat. A brother of three of our students has agreed to accompany us as we sing 'Silent Night.' They will sing one verse in Spanish, then we will all join them singing in English. This is very special because, as you may know, 'Silent Night' was first performed on a guitar. Please welcome Mr. Sandoval."

As the people clapped, our brother stood up and bowed. "Thank you. You can call me Alberto." Then he sat down, cradled the guitar, and strummed some chords for an introduction.

I held back my tears as Ernesto, Felícita, and I joined our brother, singing:

*"Noche de paz, noche de amor,*

*Todo duerme alrededor.*

*Todo el mundo celebra con fe,*

*A ese niño nacido en Belén,*

*Con canciones del corazón,*

*Hoy ha nacido el amor."*

I noticed Caroline mouthing some of the words. She had heard Alberto sing the song when we made farolitos. Maybe in the future more of our classmates might learn Spanish. Then everyone in the room sang two verses together in English.

After all the bowing and applause, Miss Shugart announced, "I'd like all the students to sit with their parents to get ready for another special guest."

Caroline followed me and we sat down by Alberto, Papá, Mamá, and Caroline's father.

"Ladies and gentlemen, our special guest has requested 'Jingle Bells,'" Miss Shugart said. "Please welcome him." She blew a note on her pitch pipe and everyone sang, "*Dashing through the snow, in a one-horse open sleigh. Over the fields we go . . .*"

Suddenly, a voice shouted, "Ho, ho, ho!" and everyone turned their heads to see a big man with a white beard bounding through the front door. He wore a bright red suit and had a large gunnysack slung over his back.

I turned to Caroline. "Is that Santa Claus?" I whispered.

"Yes, Margarita!" she said, peeking over the heads of people in back of us. I stood up to get a better look. Santa Claus's eyes twinkled just like the poem said.

He started to make his way to the head of the classroom but stopped when he saw Ernesto sitting on Papá's lap. He looked down at Ernesto over his half glasses.

"Have you been a good boy this year, Ernesto?" he said.

Ernesto's wide eyes and nod of his head answered what his mouth couldn't. How did Santa Claus know his name?

"Well, I have a present for every boy and girl," Santa Claus said, "and that includes you!" He ruffled Ernesto's hair. When he reached the front of the room, he put his big sack down. "Come on up. Now don't be shy."

"Come on," Felícita said. She took Ernesto's hand. Caroline stood up too, and they all looked at me.

"No, go ahead," I said. Papá and Alberto had their jobs. I didn't need anything more. "He already gave me a present."

Caroline cocked her head. "No, really, Margarita, there are more presents. Let's go." She pushed me out of the row to follow my sister and brother, and she was close behind.

We joined the line of our classmates, and finally it was our turn to talk to Santa Claus. "I hope you like this, Ernesto," Santa Claus said. "You and Margarita did a very good job with my poem. I could hear you as I waited to make my grand entrance."

*How does he know my name?* I wondered. *Have we met before?*

"Thank you, Santa Claus," Ernesto said. Santa gave him a small box wrapped in pretty paper along with a paper sack.

"Merry Christmas, Felícita. Here you are, Margarita." Santa Claus gave us each a wrapped box and a little brown sack too. The sack felt as heavy as our farolitos, but I doubted there was dirt in these.

"Thank you," Felícita said. She took Ernesto's hand and headed back to the bench.

"Thank you, Santa Claus," I said. "My papá and brother kept their jobs, and the people here are good to us. Thank you for everything. Merry Christmas."

"You're welcome, little lady, and Feliz Navidad to you and your family."

For a stranger, he seemed so familiar. After I sat down next to Caroline, I studied the tag on my present. It didn't say *Margaret* or even *Maggie*. It said *Margarita*.

"Can I see what Santa Claus wrote?" I asked my sister. Her tag said *Felícita*, not *Phyllis*, as the kids in school called her. When we were in line, Santa Claus hadn't looked at the tags before he talked to us, so he knew our faces as well as our real names. How did he do it?

Ernesto started to open his present.

"Wait a minute. How about if we open these in front

of Abuela, especially since she couldn't come?" I said.

"That's a good idea," said Felícita.

"Okay. I'll wait too," Ernesto said.

Our classmates tore into their presents, but Caroline crossed the room, handed her box to her grandmother, and came back, still carrying her paper bag and another box.

"I asked Grandma if I could go to your house to see you open your presents, if that's okay with you," she said.

"Sure. I was going to ask you to come over. I think we even have some biscochitos left." I put my coat on and picked up my brown paper bag. A waft of something sweet reached my nose. "This bag smells like an orange."

"I smell candy," Ernesto said.

"Maybe it's both," Caroline said.

Then we all walked to our home. It wasn't just our house—it was our *home*. This was a place I felt we belonged now.

We brought Abuela into the kitchen, and everyone gathered around the kitchen table.

"Caroline," I said, handing her a gift. "I'm glad . . . we're all glad you and your family are our friends. We made you this."

Caroline's eyes misted up as her finger traced the kitten embroidered on the tea towel. "Thank you. I love it."

"There's more," Ernesto said.

She slowly unwrapped the next present and her hand flew to her mouth. "You made this bolillo? For me?"

I nodded. "You know a Spanish word!"

She put her hands on her hips. "I know a few."

"It was kind of tricky getting your grandma to retire my favorite broom," I said. "I cut about nine inches off the handle with Papá's ax. Then I sanded it smooth so you can roll out your own tortillas."

She smiled and leaned toward me. "I wondered why we had a new broom after you had broken in the other one."

We all laughed.

"Thank you, everyone," Caroline said. "Thank you for including me in your family. I have something too . . . but it's only for Margarita." She handed me a box and I tore off the paper.

I hugged the paper dolls to my chest. "Thank you!"

"You're welcome. I know it's not a real Shirley Temple doll, but look at all the clothes you can dress Shirley in."

We both studied the two pages of clothes. It was going to be fun for Caroline and me to dress the paper doll.

"Now let's see what Santa Claus brought us," Ernesto said.

The four of us emptied our bags. There was candy that looked like a rainbow of stiff ribbons, and my orange almost rolled off the table. An orange! It had been so long since I tasted one.

"Let's eat mine first," I said.

Orange oils sprayed when I pushed my thumbs into the bittersweet skin. I separated each segment carefully so everyone could have a slice of liquid sunshine.

"It's so cold, it hurts my teeth," Ernesto said, and he shivered.

Felícita unwrapped her present. "Oh, look! *Anne of Green Gables*. I've been wanting to read this ever since Miss Shugart told us about it."

"Yippee!" Ernesto shouted as he showed Alberto a cat's-eye marble from his drawstring bag. "The eye looks like the eyes of the Kit-Cat Klock."

I opened my present. It was like the box I had seen at the Simses' store, with a picture of a little fat man with a tall black hat and the word MONOPOLY written across it. "What's this?" I asked Papá.

"It's a board game for our family," he said.

"It's a fun game, Maggie," Caroline said. I looked at her with raised eyebrows. She corrected herself: "Margarita."

I went over to Abuela and gave her the last piece of my orange. "Abuela," I said. "You must have prayed to Santo Niño and asked him if Santa Claus knew us."

She smiled and Papá laughed out loud. "Of course he knows us," Papá said.

I took the directions out of the box to see how to play the game. "Mira," I said, showing Papá the paper. "Santa

Claus *really* knows our family. He wrote the directions in Spanish!"

Papá and Mamá smiled at me and then at each other. It seemed like Papá was taller, or maybe it was just because his thumbs were lifting his suspenders.

"I can help you learn the game," said Caroline.

"Sure. That'll be fun," I said. I pointed to the gift tag. "See, Caroline. Even Santa Claus calls me Margarita!"

## CHAPTER 28

## Santa Bárbara
### INVOKED FOR THE HOME

**The next day,** Caroline met me on the playground and pointed to the thin folder I was carrying. "Is that for Miss Shugart?"

"No. Ernesto has her gifts. This is something I want to show everyone in school."

She tapped her lips. "Hmm. It can't be something to eat—it would be squashed." Her eyes lit up. "Tell me."

I laughed. "No. Just wait and see."

"Okay, okay, I'll wait." Then she leaned in. "The last day of school before vacation is always a fun day. The way it works is, when all the desks and the room are put back in order, Miss Shugart opens her gifts in front of everyone. We don't have tests, just a few lessons. We even get to draw while Miss Shugart reads to us."

As soon as Miss Shugart took attendance and we said the Pledge, all the students went to work cleaning up the school. Some took down paper chains. I laughed when I saw Ernesto jump up with his ruler to bring down a chain on the wall. The older boys carried the Christmas tree outside so the birds could eat the popcorn strands. I grabbed the broom and swept up pine needles. The older girls moved Miss Shugart's desk back to the front of the room. Everyone picked up their desks and moved them to the correct rows.

When the room was in order, Miss Shugart sat down at her desk, which was now covered with little boxes wrapped in shiny paper. I looked at Ernesto and Felícita. I hadn't realized we were supposed to put our gifts on the teacher's desk.

Before we could go up, the oldest boy and girl in the school walked to the front of the class. Joe Hancock spoke to Miss Shugart. "On behalf of some students in the eighth grade, we would like you to have these tickets to the movie theater in Rawlins."

Helen blushed. "The movie *Treasure Island* is playing now and so is *Anne of Green Gables*," she said.

Miss Shugart laughed. "Thank you. It will be hard to choose."

She opened all the gifts on her desk. She tried to guess what was in the packages the younger students brought, and they squealed when she guessed wrong. The twins in Ernesto's class gave her some homemade fudge. Another kid gave her a calendar. She received a bottle of ink and a pen from one family, popcorn balls, and enough fruit from other students to fill a basket. Finally, there were no more gifts on the desk.

I caught Ernesto and Felícita's eyes and mouthed, "Let's go up." Ernesto pulled the gifts out of his desk, and I raised my hand.

"Yes?" Miss Shugart said.

"My sister, brother, and I have gifts for you too."

Miss Shugart smiled and motioned for us to come to her desk. We probably looked like the Three Kings.

Ernesto presented her with a handkerchief Mamá had edged in blue crochet thread. "It's beautiful," she said, holding it up. "Thank you so much." She opened the box of pumpkin empanadas Felícita gave her. "I do love pumpkin," she said as she smelled them. "Did you make them?"

Felícita smiled and looked down.

As I handed Miss Shugart my little box, it rattled. She shook it near her ear.

"It's rocks," Sam said from his seat near the potbellied stove.

"Oh, I don't think they're rocks—unless they're very small," Miss Shugart said. She smelled the box. "It can't be a pine tree, but it smells like one." She took her time unwrapping it. "They're nuts, I think." She smelled them again and looked at me with questioning eyes. "What kind of nuts are these?"

"These are piñón. They grow on a special kind of tree

in New Mexico. We roasted them, so all you have to do is crack the shells with your teeth. The little nuts are white."

"I'm sure I'll enjoy them." She stood and spread her arms out wide just like a priest blessing the people. "Thank you all for these fine gifts!"

I took a deep breath. "Miss Shugart," I said, "may I share something with the school before our lessons?"

"Of course. History and geography can wait a moment."

"Well, it *is* history and geography, actually." I went to my desk to get my folder. "When the eighth graders were studying the Civil War, my sister said our great-grandfather fought in the Civil War. I brought proof that he did."

There was a buzz in the room as I opened the folder and held up the first paper from Abuelita Cruzita. "This is an enlistment record that shows our great-grandfather fought in the fourth regiment of the Union army in New Mexico." I raised it high so all the students could see it. Then I took out the second page. "This shows that our great-grandmother received a pension because her husband, our great-grandfather, fought in the war." I held the paper up as far as my arms would reach and slowly turned my body. "I won't pass them around because they're old, but you can come up later and look at them on Miss Shugart's desk."

Miss Shugart adjusted her glasses and looked at one

of the papers. "My lands. I learn something every day. I did not realize the Civil War was fought this far west. That's what I get for going to school back east." She looked at the eighth-grade students and put her hand on her chest. "I apologize for the incorrect information I led you to believe."

"Are there any questions?" I asked.

Joe Hancock raised his hand and stood up, almost knocking his desk over. "Why would people from Mexico fight in our Civil War? They're from another country."

I felt myself get warm and noticed both of Caroline's hands waving.

"Yes, Caroline," Miss Shugart said.

She stood up and pointed to herself. "Joe, you and I haven't learned United States geography very well. In fact, there are adults in this town who don't know their geography either. Margarita's family is from *New Mexico*, a state that fought for the Union, not Mexico, which is a different country."

"Thank you, Caroline," Miss Shugart said.

I nodded at the rolled-up map hanging on the wall. "May I?"

Miss Shugart leaned in. "Of course."

I carefully pulled the string down so the map would stay in place. "Raise your hand if you know how many states there are and how many stars are on the flag," I said, pointing to the flag by the door.

All the hands in the classroom went up and I called on Ernesto's friend Sam.

He stood up. "Forty-eight stars and forty-eight states."

I picked up Miss Shugart's pointer stick. "Correct." I tapped New Mexico on the map. "Before it became a state, different flags flew over New Mexico. First the Spanish flag, then the Mexican flag, and last—the American flag. New Mexico became the forty-seventh state in 1912."

I pointed to myself, my sister, and brother. "We moved from New Mexico this year, but our Spanish ancestors moved there in 1598. They gave thanks on this land before the *Mayflower* pilgrims had their Thanksgiving." I put the pointer stick down and walked back to my seat.

Miss Shugart stood up and clapped, and soon everyone in the room was clapping too. "Thank you for that informative history and geography lesson. We're so glad the Sandoval family is part of our school and town. I'm sure you'll continue to teach everyone about your long heritage from the state of . . ."

She put her hand to her ear, and my classmates in one voice said, "New Mexico!"

Miss Shugart was right. We were a part of the school, just as our family was part of Fort Steele. New Mexico would always be home in my heart, but now we had a new home in Wyoming.

# Author's Note

*The Wind Called My Name* is loosely based on my mother's life, and on the lives and stories of both sides of my family. Unlike Margarita in my novel, my mother, Margarita Lucia Sandoval, was born in Fort Steele, Wyoming, in 1928. My grandfather, Filadelfio Sandoval, worked on the section, and my grandmother, Josefita (Maes) Sandoval, tended to her family and a large garden. My mother's older siblings—Alberto, Trevino José, Rufina, Elighio, and Felícita—were born in New Mexico. Her younger brother, Ernesto, was also born in Fort Steele.

When my mother was a girl, her main job was to tend to her blind grandmother, Rufina (Maldonado) Maes, who told many stories about her own life. My great-grandmother was baptized in Arroyo Seco near Taos, New Mexico in 1848 by the infamous rebel priest Antonio José Martínez. (Martínez was later portrayed as a villain in the novel *Death Comes to the Archbishop* by Willa Cather.) While I never met my great-grandmother Rufina, I did know my mother's paternal grandmother, Cruzita (Cardenas) Sandoval. When we visited her in the small village of El Carmen, New Mexico, she milked a goat and gave us fresh milk to drink. She became blind later in life, and I can still picture her rolling homemade cigarettes made from loose tobacco in a Prince Albert can.

My mother did write a fan letter to Shirley Temple in the 1930s, and at one school Christmas party, she received a game with instructions in Spanish as described in the novel (though it was not a Monopoly game). She always said the instructions proved to her that Santa Claus was real.

My father, William Gonzales, was born in Chacon, New Mexico in 1927, and moved with his father, José Adelaido Gonzales, and mother, Beroníz (Lovato) Gonzales, to Tipton, Wyoming in 1943. He left behind his beloved dog, as Margarita does in the story. My grandfather worked on the section for the Union Pacific Railroad, as did my uncle, Levi Efrén, and even my dad during his first summer in Wyoming. My younger uncle, Manuel, delivered newspapers, which were thrown from the train, while my aunt Mary loved to play with paper dolls. The family later moved to Rawlins, Wyoming, where my parents met and married in 1945.

Even though I was born and raised in Rawlins, my Hispanic community was tied together by our northern New Mexican roots and close family connections. We knew the names of many of our ancestors, and daily experienced the traditions of the people who colonized the northernmost area of New Spain—today known as New Mexico. I can distinctly remember a family matanza where my grandfather slaughtered a sheep and we cousins watched the steam rise from the grass that was in the sheep's stomach. The women made burrañates and menudo, and the huge curved ribs filled the oven. The long sheep's head was in the refrigerator for another meal of scrambled eggs and brains. Many people of the New Mexican diaspora feel a querencia, or desire and yearning, for our familial home, and I do too.

New Mexico has a complicated history. In 1598, about four hundred Spanish colonizers and Native servants or enslaved people crossed over the Río Grande from present-day Mexico and advanced up to what is now northern New Mexico. They arrived at a Tewa pueblo called Ohkay Owingeh, which the colonists renamed San Juan de los Caballeros. The colonists were under the leadership of a man named Juan de Oñate, who sought gold and treasure and punished those who challenged his rule. Over the next eight years, Oñate and his followers explored and settled territory as far northeast as Oklahoma and as far west as the Gulf of California. In order to survive in this new land, the colonists depended on many different Pueblo nations to teach them new ways of farming and other life skills. The Pueblo in turn adopted some of the food, plants, livestock, and farm implements the colonists had brought from Mexico. The combination of Puebloan practices and the colonists' Spanish language, music, art, and Catholic faith and traditions created a new and unique cultural landscape in the region. At the same time, Oñate and other colonizers killed or enslaved hundreds of Native people, particularly at the Acoma Pueblo. He was eventually summoned back to the Spanish capital in Mexico City and tried and banished for his cruelty.

Even though the Native people had lived on New Mexican land for centuries, these colonists planted their Spanish flag over it. The two cultures coexisted but also fought with one another until the Native Americans were able to expel the Spanish in 1680, only for the Spanish to return in 1693 with even more colonists. In 1821, Mexico gained its independence from Spain, and the Mexican flag flew over the area. Then in 1848, after the Mexican-American War, the land was taken over by the United States government and the American flag appeared. Today, twenty-three Native American nations remain sovereign states in New Mexico, including nineteen Pueblos, three Apache nations, and the Navajo Nation.

In 1865, after the Civil War erupted, one of my great-great-grandfathers, José del Carmel Cardenas, volunteered to fight for the Union. I was able to find preserved archival records that show he served as a private in the United States of America Volunteer regiment of the 1st New Mexico Calvary, Company F.

Growing up, I knew my family's stories orally, but I never saw a written story about our culture. Then, in my children's literature class at the University of Wyoming, we read Newbery Award–winning books, and that's when I discovered ... *And Now Miguel* by Joseph Krumgold. The setting was the Sangre de Cristo Mountains near Taos, New Mexico, where Miguel herded his family's sheep in the mountains, just as my father had done. After that experience, I have made it a lifelong quest to read books about my colonial New Mexican heritage and to search for other authors of Hispanic and Latinx descent.

I wrote the original draft of this story about twenty years ago as a Christmas gift for my mother, celebrating her life as a child. Then in 2005, I met acclaimed author Rudolfo Anaya, a Hispanic writer from New Mexico. He was promoting his children's book *The Santero's Miracle* and autographed it to me with these words: *Believe in miracles! I'll wait for your stories.* Around that time I also took a writing class from Matt de la Peña. These authors inspired me to work to get my story out to a bigger audience than just my family.

The Hispanic culture is rich in diversity all over the world. I hope I have given you a glimpse into my unique culture, which has flourished in the United States for over four hundred years. My bigger hope is that you are motivated to write the story only you can write. As children's author Isabel Campo says, "There is room for seven billion stories, one written by each person on this tiny planet."

# List of Dichos

*The dichos are taken from* Refranes: Southwestern Spanish Proverbs, *collected and translated by Rubén Cobos (Santa Fe: Museum of New Mexico Press, 1985).*

**Al amigo y al caballo, no cansarlos.** Tire out neither your friend nor your horse.

**Al que se ayuda, Dios le ayuda.** God helps those who help themselves.

**Amigo en la adversidad, amigo de verdad.** A friend in need is a friend indeed.

**Cuando el dinero habla, todos callan.** When money talks, everyone shuts up.

**Cuando hace viento, quédate adentro.** When it's windy, stay indoors.

**Cuando ven un pobre caído todos le dan con el pie.** When people see a poor man down, everyone kicks him.

**El hogar es donde cuelgas tu sombrero.** Home is where you hang your hat.

**El que adelante no mira, atrás se queda.** He who doesn't look ahead stays behind.

**Gracia es andar entre las llamas y no quermarse.** The trick is to walk among the flames and not get burned.

**La verdad, aunque severa, es amiga verdadera.** The truth, while harsh, is a good friend.

**Más vale un amigo que mil parientes, ellos lejos y él presente.** A friend close by is worth a thousand relatives far away.

**No donde naces, sino donde paces.** It's not where you were born, but where you're spending your time.

**Quien la fama ha perdido, está muerto aunque vivo.** Literally, "He who loses his reputation is as good as dead though he may be alive," meaning "He who takes away my good name takes away my life."

**Panza llena, corazón contento.** Full belly, happy heart.

**Un buen gallo en cualquier gallinero canta.** A good rooster sings in any roost.

**Unos cardan la lana y otros agarran la fama.** Some card the wool and others grab the credit.

# Glossary and Pronunciation Guide

*Words originally from Spanish include their northern New Mexican pronunciations.*

**abuela, abuelita** (ah-BWEH-lah, ah-bweh-LEE-tah): grandmother, little grandmother (a term of endearment)

**abuelo** (ah-BWEH-loh): grandfather

**acequias** (ah-SEH-kee-ahs): aqueducts, or long ditches dug to carry water from one place to another

**Act of Contrition**: a special prayer in the Catholic Church to express sorrow for one's sins

**adiós** (ah-DTHOHS): goodbye

**adobe** (ah-DOH-beh): a kind of desert clay that is mixed with straw to create bricks; also, structures made from such bricks, which are found throughout the American Southwest

**ahora** (ah-OH-rah): now

**amiga** (ah-ME-gah): friend (female)

**Arapaho**: a Native American nation that has historically dwelt on the plains of Colorado and Wyoming

**atole flour** (ah-TOH-lay): flour made from blue corn

**"Ay, qué bueno"** (Eye, keh BWEH-noh): "Oh, how good."

**barracks**: a building or group of buildings used to house soldiers

**Battle of Valverde** (vahl-VEHR-deh): a February 1862 Civil War battle in New Mexico Territory, where the Confederates claimed victory but suffered heavy casualties

**Battle of Glorieta Pass**: a March 1862 Civil War battle that became the turning point of the fight in New Mexico Territory; after the Union won, the Confederates were forced to withdraw to Arizona

**Big Chief**: a brand of notebook that featured a stereotypical image of a Native American chief on the front cover

**bisabuelo** (bees-ah-BWEH-loh): great-grandfather

**biscochitos** (bees-koh-CHEE-tohs): crispy cookies with anise flavoring; the state cookie of New Mexico

**Bisquick:** a brand of pancake and baking mix

**bolillo** (boh-LEE-yoh): in northern New Mexico, a thin rolling pin

**bueno** (BWEH-noh): good

**Buenos días te/le de Dios** (BWEH-nohs DEE-ahs teh/leh deh DTHOHS): good morning; *te* is used for people with whom the speaker is familiar, and *le* is used when the speaker wishes to speak more respectfully

**Buenas noches** (BWEH-nahs NO-chehs): good night

**burrito** (boo-RREE-toh): flour tortilla filled with meat, beans, and/or cheese

**burrañates** (boo-rrah-NYAH-tehs): the small intestines of a lamb, which are cut into pieces, wrapped around long pieces of lard, and baked in the oven

**calabacitas** (cah-lah-bah-SEE-tahs): little green pumpkins or squashes

**camposanto** (cam-poh-SAHN-toh): cemetery

**capulín** (cah-pooh-LEEN): chokecherry, a kind of tree which produces berries that make excellent jelly

**Cheyenne:** the state capital of Wyoming

**chicharrónes** (chee-chah-RROH-nehs): crispy fried pork skins

**chicos** (CHEE-kohs): dried corn put in soups

**chile** (CHEE-leh): spicy red or green peppers; if you want to taste both in New Mexican restaurants, request your chile "Christmas style"

**chile caribe** (CHEE-leh cah-REE-beh): coarsely ground dried red chile

**chile colorado** (CHEE-leh koh-loh-RAH-thdo) a gravy-like dish made by browning flour in fat to make a roux, then adding red chile powder and water

**chile pequín** (CHEE-leh peh-KEEN): tiny hot dried chile peppers and their seeds, used as a spice and in some salsas

**chile verde** (CHEE-leh VEHR-deh): fresh green roasted and peeled chile, often put in chile stew

**cigarro** (see-GAH-rroh): a cigar

**claro que sí** (CLAH-ro keh see): of course

**Claudette:** Alberto's car is named for Claudette Colbert, an actress who appeared in many famous films in the 1930s, including *It Happened One Night* with Clark Gable

**cobija** (co-BEE-hah): blanket

**comal** (coh-MALL): a small cast-iron disk or flat pan used to cook tortillas

**Communion:** a rite of Christian worship in which bread and wine are shared with the congregation

**compadre** (com-PAH-dreh): a special friend who is connected to the family through a marriage or baptism

**con mucho amor** (con MOO-choh ah-MOR): with much love

**con mucho gusto** (con MOO-choh GOOSE-toh): with great pleasure

**Creo que es una oportunidad** (KREH-oh keh ess OO-nah oh-poor-too-nee-DAHD): I think it is an opportunity.

**Depression, the**: often called the Great Depression; a period of severe economic hardship in the United States, lasting from about 1929-1939, during which millions of people were out of work

**Devils Tower**: a tower of igneous rock that stands 867 feet tall on the northeastern plains of Wyoming. It is sacred to several Native American tribes and was named the first US National Monument in 1906.

**dicho** (DEE-choh): a common saying, like a proverb

**dime** (DEE-meh): tell me

**Dime lo que ves** (DEE-meh loh keh vehz): tell me what you see

**Donald Duck**: an early Disney cartoon character

**Dutch oven**: a thick-walled cooking pot

**Eddie Cantor**: the host of a popular radio variety show that introduced the song "Santa Claus is Comin' to Town" in November 1934

**embarazada** (em-bah-rah-ZAH-dah): pregnant

**empanaditas** (em-pah-nah-DEE-tahs): little turnovers stuffed with meat and seasonings or fruits

**enchiladas** (en-chee-LAH-dahs): rolled tortilla filled with cheese and sometimes beef or chicken and baked covered in sauce

**¿Entiendes?** (en-TYEN-dehs): Do you understand?

**En el nombre del Padre, y del Hijo, y del Espíritu Santo** (en elle NOM-breh dehl PAH-dreh, ee dehl EE-ho, ee dehl ess-PEE-ree-too SAHN-toh): In the name of the Father, and the Son, and the Holy Spirit

**Es su nombre en la escuela** (Ess soo NOM-breh en lah ess-KWEH-lah): It's her name in school.

**Es un santo** (ess oon SAHN-toh): He is a saint.

**escuela** (ess-KWEH-lah): school

**familia** (fah-MEE-lyah): family

**Famous Funnies**: a 1934 collection of comic strips now considered the first modern comic book

**farolitos** (fah-roh-LEE-tohs): lantern-like lights made by nestling and lighting votive candles in small sand-filled paper bags to symbolically light the way for the Holy Family on Christmas Eve. These are known as *luminarias* in other parts of the world, but they are called *farolitos* in northern New Mexico.

**fedora**: a hat with a wide brim and an indented crown

**Feliz Navidad** (feh-LEES nah-vee-DAHD): Merry Christmas

**FERA**: the Federal Employment Relief Association, a government program that lasted from 1933 to 1935 and created millions of jobs for Americans put out of work by the Great Depression.

**Flash Gordon**: a comic strip about a man named Flash Gordon and his adventures on the planet Mongo, which ran in newspapers from 1934 to 2003

**Gable, Clark**: a movie star of the 1930s and 1940s, famous for his roles in *It Happened One Night*, *Gone With the Wind*, and many other films

**gente** (HEN-teh): people

**Georgia:** Georgia O'Keeffe, an American painter who is especially known for her pictures of flowers and the American Southwest

**gracias** (GRAH-syahs): thank you

**gracias a Dios** (GRAH-syahs ah DTHOHS): thanks to God

**gringos** (GREEN-gohs): Americans of European but non-Hispanic descent

**gunny sack**: an inexpensive bag made of burlap

**Hace mucho tiempo** (AH-seh mooh-CHOH TYEM-poh): It's been a long time

**Hail Mary**: a Catholic prayer to the Virgin Mary that traditionally begins, "Hail Mary, full of grace, the Lord is with thee; blessed art thou amongst women, and blessed is the fruit of thy womb, Jesus"

**hasta el cielo** (AHS-tah elle see-EH-loh): until heaven

**hava beans** (AH-vah): broad beans in fuzzy pods

**Hay más piñón** (aye mahs pee-NYOHN): There is more piñón.

**Heidi:** the main character in the 1881 novel *Heidi* by Johanna Spyri, about a girl who grows up on a mountain in the Swiss Alps. Shirley Temple starred in a 1937 film adaptation.

**hija, hijita** (EE-hah, ee-HEE-tah): daughter, little daughter (a term of endearment)

**hijo, hijito** (EE-hoh, ee-HEE-toh): son, little son

**Holmes, Sherlock**: a fictional detective who appears in many novels and short stories by Sir Arthur Conan Doyle

**Holy Family**: Joseph, Mary, and baby Jesus

**hominy**: soup made from dried corn treated with alkali

**host**: in the Communion rite, the piece of bread that represents Jesus's body

**huevos** (WEH-vohs): eggs

**icebox**: a refrigerator with no motor

**intercede**: to get involved in a situation with the intention of resolving differences

**invoke**: to call on someone in prayer

IOU: a paper stating the debt one person owes to another, or an "I owe you"

**KePeg**: a natural egg preserver developed during the Great Depression; it closed the pores of eggshells to preserve the interior of the egg and could keep an egg from spoiling without refrigeration

**kerosene**: lamp oil

**Kit-Cat Klock**: a popular model of clock, first made in 1932, where the clock sits in the stomach of a cartoon cat and its eyes and tail move back and forth with the seconds

**Laramie**: a city in Wyoming

**Lent**: in the Christian religious calendar, the period of forty weekdays between Ash Wednesday and Easter

**linen**: a fine cloth made from flax

*Little Miss Marker*: a 1934 film directed by Alexander Hall and starring Shirley Temple, Adolphe Menjou, and Dorothy Dell

**Little Orphan Annie**: the heroine of a long-running comic strip about an orphan girl with curly red hair who went to live with rich Daddy Warbucks

**llanos** (YAH-nohs): plains

**La Llorona** (la yoh-ROH-nah): the Weeping Woman, a character in Mexican folklore whose eternal penance for having drowned her children is to try to find them, and who is said to carry off children who misbehave

**loco / loca** (LOH-koh / LOH-kah): crazy (masculine/feminine)

**luminarias** (loo-mee-NAHR-ee-ahs): bonfires built to symbolically light the way for the Holy Family on Christmas Eve

**madrina** (mah-DREE-nah): a woman who is a sponsor at a baptism or wedding

**Las Mañanitas** (lahs mah-nyah-NEE-tahs): a traditional birthday or saint's day song in many Latin American countries

**más despacio** (mahs dehs-PAH-syo): more slowly

**mason jars**: clear glass jars first created by John Landis Mason to preserve food during the canning process

**Mass:** a Catholic religious service

**matanza** (mah-TAHN-zah): literally, slaughter; a community gathering where an animal is slaughtered and butchered to share among the attendees

**mayordomo** (my-or-DOH-moh): boss; the boss who oversees the clearing of the acequias in New Mexico

**mejicanos** (meh-hee-CAH-nohs): Mexicans

**Mentholatum:** a brand of skin ointment that gave relief to sore muscles and joints

**menudo** (meh-NOO-doh): a stew made with tripe and chiles

**Mexican-American War**: an armed conflict that lasted from 1846-1848 between the United States and Mexico, concluded by a treaty that required Mexico to cede all or portions of present-day Arizona, California, Colorado, Nevada, New Mexico, Utah, and Wyoming to the United States, and established a new border between the countries at the Río Grande river

**m'ijo** (MEE-ho): my son (a contraction of *mi* and *hijo*)

**Mira** (MEE-rah): Look.

**Mis Crismes** (mees CREES-mehs): a tradition like Halloween where Hispanic children in New Mexico and southern Colorado go around the neighborhood on Christmas morning, asking for Christmas goodies

**Monopoly**: a board game created and popularized by Charles Darrow, based on *The Landlord's Game* by Elizabeth Magie Phillips

**Montgomery Ward**: a company that sold a wide range of goods through its stores and catalog

**morcilla** (moor-SEE-yah): a type of sausage made from the blood of a slaughtered pig

**muy** (muee): very

**New York Giants**: one of the first Major League Baseball teams, founded in New York City in 1883; they moved across the country and became the San Francisco Giants in 1958

**nichos** (NEE-chohs): niches, or small indentations cut into walls to hold statues or other precious items

**niño, niños** (NEEN-yoh, NEEN-yohs): child, children (boys or mixed boys and girls)

**niña, niñas** (NEEN-yah, NEEN-yahs): girl, girls

**No llores** (no YO-rehs): Don't cry.

**Noche Buena** (NO-cheh BWEH-nah): Christmas Eve

**Noche de Paz** (NO-cheh deh pahs): Night of Peace; the Spanish name for the song "Silent Night"

**nombre** (NOM-breh): name

**Nuestra casa es su casa** (NWEHS-trah CAH-sah ess soo CAH-sah): Our house is your house.

**Nuestra Señora de los Dolores** (NWEHS-trah seh-NYOH-rah deh lohs doh-LOH-rehs): Our Lady of Sorrows; another name for the Virgin Mary

**Old Faithful**: a famous hot geyser in Yellowstone Park in Wyoming, which erupts every forty-four to one hundred twenty-five minutes

**Oñate, Juan de** (oh-NYAH-teh, hoo-an deh): a controversial Spanish conquistador who explored, colonized, and governed northern New Spain, later known as New Mexico, from 1598 to 1607

**Ovaltine**: a brand of hot drink made with cocoa

**outhouse**: an outdoor toilet in a small hut

**padre** (PAH-dreh): a Catholic priest

**padrino** (pah-DREE-noh): a man who is a sponsor at a baptism or wedding

**para** (PAH-rah): for

**patron saint**: a special saint invoked for specific intentions by a person or a community

**penance**: an outward act of repentance (often, in the Catholic church, a specific prayer)

**peperoncino:** Italian name for spicy chile flakes and seeds

**pero** (PEH-roh): but

**Peter Rabbit:** a generic name for rabbits, based on Beatrix Potter's series of children's books starring the character

**pinafore:** a sleeveless apron-like garment worn over a child's dress

**piñón** (pee-NYOHN): small brown pine nuts from a specific pine tree species. In New Mexican dialect, "piñón" can be both singular and plural.

**por** (por): for

**por favor** (por fah-VOR): please

**Las Posadas** (lahs poh-SAH-dahs): literally, "the lodgings"; a holiday celebrated from December 16-24 in many Hispanic and Latinx communities, reenacting the part of the Christmas story in which Mary and Joseph search for lodging in Bethlehem

**Las Posadas es buena para nuestra familia** (lahs poh-SAH-dahs ess BWEH-nah PAH-rah NWEH-stra fah-MEE-lyah): Las Posadas is good for our family.

**posole** (poh-SOH-leh): a type of hominy stew made from corn, meat, and chile

**primo / prima** (PREE-moh / PREE-mah): cousin (male/female)

**purty:** country slang for *pretty*

**Qué bonito** (keh boh-NEE-toh): How beautiful.

**¿Qué es esto?** (keh ess ESS-toh): What is this?

**¿Qué pasó?** (keh PAH-so): What happened?

**Qué linda** (keh LEEN-dah): How pretty.

**quelites** (keh-LEE-tehs): a kind of wild green, like spinach; often called lamb's quarters

**querencia** (keh-REN-sya): love and yearning for a special place

**¿Quién es?** (KEEYEN ess): Who is . . . ?

**railroaders:** men who work on the railroad

**Rawlins:** the county seat of Carbon County, Wyoming, about seventeen miles west of Fort Steele; the Ferris Mansion, Hugus-Ferguson building, and Strand Theater (Fox Theater) are real historical buildings and can still be seen there

**Recuerdo cuando nacieron tú y Alberto** (reh-KWER-thdoh KWAN-doh nah-CYER-on tu ee al-BEAR-toh): I remember when you and Alberto were born.

**Recuerdas eso** (reh-KWER-dahs EH-so): Remember that.

**retablos** (reh-TAH-blohs): small religious paintings on wood or metal

**Río Grande blanket** (REE-oh GRAN-deh): a wool blanket created from naturally dyed fibers by Hispanic weavers in New Mexico

**ristra** (REESE-trah): a string of many green chiles, which turn red when hung to dry

**rosary:** a string of beads used for ritual prayer in the Catholic Church

**San Sebastián** (SAHN seh-bahs-TIAN): an early Christian saint who was shot with many arrows; invoked for a holy death, and by archers and athletes

**santo / santa** (SAHN-toh / SAHN-tah): saint (masculine/feminine)

**Santo Niño de Atocha** (SAHN-toh NEEN-yo deh ah-TOH-chah): the patron saint of prisoners, because legend says the Christ child appeared as a pilgrim in Spain carrying food in a basket to Christian prisoners, and the basket continued to be full even after they ate

**Sawyer, Tom**: the hero of *The Adventures of Tom Sawyer*, a novel by Mark Twain

**señor** (seh-NYOR): mister, sir

**señora** (seh-NYO-rah): missus, madam

**señorita** (seh-nyo-REE-tah): miss

**Seventh-day Adventists**: a Protestant Christian church denomination established in the mid-1860s, known for celebrating the Sabbath on Saturday

**sí** (SEE): yes

**"Silent Night"**: a Christmas carol first performed in Oberndorf, Germany, on December 24, 1818, by its lyricist, Joseph Mohr, and composer, Franz Gruber, who sang it together with Mohr's accompaniment on guitar

**Spam:** canned food made from pork meat and ham

**spittoon:** a vaselike receptacle into which people spit chewing tobacco juice

**Su mamá era mi prima** (soo mah-MAH EH-rah mee PREE-mah): Your mama was my cousin.

**sueño** (SWEH-nyo): dream; sleepy

**suspenders:** straps that go over the shoulders and attach to trousers to hold them up

**tamales** (tah-MAH-lehs): a dish made of ground cornmeal dough filled with meat and chile, wrapped in dried corn husks, and then steamed

**Taos** (taows): a town in northern New Mexico

**Temple, Shirley**: a child actress of the 1930s who became one of Hollywood's biggest box-office stars thanks to films like *Little Miss Marker*, *Curly Top*, *The Littlest Rebel*, and *Wee Willie Winkie*

**Ten fe** (tehn feh): Have faith.

**Tenga cuidado** (TEHN-gah kwee-DAH-doh): Take care.

**Tengo un regalo** (TEHN-goh oon reh-GAH-loh): I have a gift.

**Three Kings**: the three Magi, or Wise Men, who brought the baby Jesus gifts of gold, frankincense, and myrrh

**tía** (TEE-ah): aunt

**tío** (TEE-oh): uncle

**torta de huevos** (TOR-tah deh WEH-vohs): a traditional dish with a deep-fried egg patty, somewhat like an omelet, topped with red chile gravy

**Traígame agua, por favor** (TRY-gah-meh ah-GWAH, por fah-VOR): Bring me water, please.

**Union Pacific**: one of the companies that built the first railroad to cross the entire continental United States

**Ute:** a Native American nation that has historically dwelt in the area that is now Utah, Colorado, and New Mexico

**Vaya con Dios** (VAH-yah con DTHOS): Go with God

**Victrola:** a record player

**viejitos** (vyeh-HEE-tohs): elderly people

**vinagre** (vee-NAH-greh): vinegar

**la Virgen** (la VEER-hen): the Virgin Mary, mother of Jesus

**"A Visit from Saint Nicholas"**: also known as "'Twas the Night before Christmas," this famous poem is most commonly attributed to Clement Clark Moore and established many of the traditions commonly associated with Santa Claus

**Worland:** a town in Wyoming

**y** (ee): and

**Ya me voy a Wyoming** (yah meh voy ah Wyoming): I'm going to Wyoming.

**Yo sé** (yoh seh): I know.

# Acknowledgments

Saints are ordinary people who have done extraordinary things. I consider these people, who have been and are now in my life, part of my community of saints. I'm thankful for all these saints, and for the resources and love they've given that have helped me tell this story.

The Society of Children's Book Writers and Illustrators is an advocate for all children's writers and illustrators. They actively seek diverse writers through their On-The-Verge Emerging Voices Award. Thank you to Sue Ganz-Schmitt and Martin Schmitt for funding the award. This book was made possible in part by this 2012 grant from SCBWI. They also made it possible for me to have a helpful mentor saint by my side—Chris Eboch—and the company of these Emerging Voices saints so far: Sandra Heading, Alex Brown, Tiemdow Phumiruk, Jennifer Baker, Adria Quiñones, Heidi Kim, Jackie Dorothy, Judy Allen Dodson, Collette Childers, Sindhu Vijayasarathy, Anuradha D. Rajurkar, and Lakita Wilson.

Highlights Foundation is another organization that supports children's book authors. I'm grateful for all your assistance and look forward to more opportunities to attend your workshops.

Thank you to Nicholas Scott and the Carbon County Historical Society and Museum in Rawlins, Wyoming, for researching some details and sharing them with me. Libraries also made this writing journey possible because of all the fine writing craft books and the great body of children's literature housed there that I was fortunate to read.

Children's book authors: Your stories continue to transform me. My critique groups have had the hard task of helping a novice writer grow. Kelly Dyksterhouse, Kristi Helvig, Linda Hurst,

Joanne Linden, and Jeanne Ryan, you were my first writing teachers who helped put my learning into practice. Thank you for sharing your publishing journeys. They motivated me. I continue to receive support and sound advice from new writing sisters: Shirleen Helfrick, Robin Korb, Elizabeth Junner McLaughlin, and Kathy McMahon. Your outstanding writing humbles me, and I know your time will come soon.

Thank you, Lee & Low Books, for your vision to publish stories from diverse voices, and for pairing me with editor Cheryl Klein. She should be canonized as a living saint for writers. Others on the Lee & Low Books team who deserve credit for helping to make my book the best it can be are Stacy Whitman, Tu Books publisher; Jody Corbett, a remarkable copyeditor; Christine Kettner, the book designer; and the marketing team of Hannah Ehrlich, Jalissa Corrie, and Keilin Huang. Thank you for giving me a much-needed Spanish-language review by having Alicia Ramírez double-check my grammar and overuse of accents! I'm grateful that Raúl Colón joined the team to illustrate the beautiful book cover, and my husband, Arthur, cut a colonial design on a linoleum block, which became the rosette that graces each chapter heading.

Besides the children's book community, I'm grateful for the genealogy community—especially those who highlight the Hispano experience. You planted a seed in me to tell the stories of our gente. Another community is my ancient and present Roman Catholic church community, which has given me a rich culture to draw on and continues to help me grow in my faith.

Some other people whom I have been blessed to have in my lives are my former teachers, students, co-teachers, teacher/librarian colleagues, and friends—especially Donna and Sue. You have touched and continue to touch my heart.

Events with uncles, aunts, cousins, and grandparents gave me lasting memories and stories of our family and of our ancestors. Thank you, Uncle Manuel and Aunt Phyllis, for your help with the traditional northern New Mexican Spanish, and for clarifying and expanding my memories of people and events.

I thank my parents for giving me and my sisters and brothers—Jeanie, Tim, Beverly, and Pat—our rich and proud heritage, a sense of purpose, and belief in ourselves, which carried me through the inception of this story to the end. Also, thank you for believing in me, and thanks, Pat, for the Union Pacific Railroad information.

Thank you to my children, Glenn, Greg, Natalie, and Philip, for your love and support, and for Jennifer, Kimberly, Tepe, and Nicole, who helped bring eight special young people into my life: Isabelle, Emily, Ally, Trent, Audrey, Teya, Ander, and Piper.

If there ever was a living saint, it's my husband, Arthur. Thank you for helping me pursue my passions, and for designing the beautiful rosette on each chapter heading. But most of all, thank you for enriching my life every day and showing me what heaven on earth means.

# About the Author

Mary Louise Sanchez was born and raised in Rawlins, Wyoming, not far from the setting of *The Wind Called My Name*. The manuscript for *The Wind Called My Name* won the SCBWI On-the-Verge Emerging Voices Award as well as the Tu Books New Visions Award. A retired schoolteacher/librarian, Mary Louise lives with her husband in Thornton, Colorado. Please visit her website at marylouisesanchez.com.